THE BRAINTRUST: A HARMONY OF ENEMIES

THE BRAINTRUST BOOK ONE

MARC STIEGLER

For Annette,

Welcome to the

Brain Trust

Marc Stiegler

Sept. 25, 2018

DISRUPTIVE IMAGINATION

LMBPN Publishing
PMB 196, 2540 South Maryland Pkwy
Las Vegas, NV 89109

First US Edition, December 2017
Version 1.02 August, 2018

ISBN: 978-1-64202-001-4

ACKNOWLEDGMENTS

Here's a shout-out to a few of the people who helped me with this story: Dyah Laksmi who did not save me from dengue fever, Karla Kay, who managed to read all the way through an early half-baked version of the novel, Andrew Pool with his invaluable guidance on the speech habits of terrorists, Michael Anderle who introduced me to the arcane new truths about publishing in the 21st Century, and Rosie Smith and Robin Hanson, who reminded me what I should be doing on this turn of the wheel. I hope the final novel fulfills at least some of your desires and expectations.

DEDICATION

With love and laughter, for Lynne

**The Braintrust: A Harmony of Enemies
Team Includes**

JIT Beta Readers - My deepest gratitude!

Erika Daly
Paul Westman
Joshua Ahles
Kelly ODonnell
Alex Wilson
James Caplan

*If I missed anyone, **please** let me know!*

Editor
Lynne Stiegler

BEST FRIENDS FOREVER

If the American spirit fails, what hope has the world?
—Calvin Coolidge, Dedication of the Liberty Memorial at Kansas City, Missouri

She awakened in excited anticipation again; the excitement had been building for several days. Tomorrow they would arrive at the BrainTrust by late afternoon.

The BrainTrust. So many possibilities, such wildly varying descriptions. The physical description was straightforward: an artificial island archipelago comprised of interconnected cruise liners. But beyond the simple physical description, there was so much more. Some disparaged it as a huge college dormitory jammed with over one hundred thousand overeager graduate students. Others heralded it as the last stand of the creative human spirit. Still others convincingly argued it was just a bunch of big floating sardine cans. But her favorite description was this: a vast research lab where the freedom to innovate was sacrosanct.

So many new things had come from there. Dr. Dyah Ambarawati vowed once more that she too would be one of the contributors to that flow of ever-better solutions. Surrounded by the supremely sharp people of the Brain-Trust, she could not expect to be among the smartest, but she would certainly be among the most determined.

Changes in the feel of the air and an increase in the chaotic rocking of the ship beneath her feet told her they were about to encounter a storm. She braced her elbow against the mirror to fix her lipstick as she had learned to do over the course of the last several days. This time the incipient storm rocked her backward, then slammed her forward again into the mirror. Her lipstick slipped, leaving a smear of Bobbi Brown Parisian Red across her cheek. She used a tissue to remove the smear, wondering idly if it would be easier to put lipstick on her whole face and just remove it from where it didn't belong.

Then she heard the urgent knock on the door to her cabin. "Please come in," she said in a firm tone that projected without yelling. She spoke slowly and carefully. Bahasa Indonesia was her native language, and crisp enunciation seemed to help people understand her English better.

The door squeaked as it opened, and the captain looked at her with flustered concern. "Dr. Ambara..." The captain's voice drifted off as he fumbled over her name.

She smiled and offered the nickname with which her

recently-acquired best friends had christened her. "Call me 'Dash.'"

The captain looked relieved. "Thank you, Dr. Dash." The urgency returned. "We have a young woman giving birth. It's…it's going badly. I was hoping—"

Dash swept across the cabin to her closet and pulled out her hard-used, antiquated medical bag. She slipped her arms into a white lab coat; she'd wondered why she'd brought the old thing with her, since she was going to get new ones when she got to the BrainTrust. She certainly hadn't planned to do any surgery on the ferry, even if it was a seven-day journey eastward across the Pacific from Ho Chi Minh City. Now she knew why she'd brought it. She *would* in fact be performing surgery here, on a ship that rocked as it cut through the water. She rushed down the passageway, urging the captain to hurry as they ran toward the First Aid Compartment.

The young woman was dying. Her labor was difficult all right, but that was not the problem. She was gasping for air, to no avail.

Dash was investigating possible causes when she saw a flicker on the conferencing screen on the far wall in her peripheral vision. A woman's voice emanated from it. "Dr. Ambarawati, I'm Dr. Copeland aboard the BrainTrust." At that Dash looked up in surprise. The pale face of a middle-aged Caucasian with short white hair and blue eyes gazed back at her. "Dr. Copeland, how nice to meet you. Thank you for accepting my research proposal. We have a serious problem here." As she spoke, she realized what the problem was. "Amniotic fluid embolism," she said sharply as a wave rocked the ship.

The woman on the screen looked skeptical, "That's very rare. Very unlikely. What evidence brought you to that diagnosis?"

"Several items. First —" she stopped speaking as the image on the screen flickered out. "Middle of the ocean," Dash muttered to herself. "Rain-fade on the Ka-band. It was a miracle she got through at all."

Dash needed to intubate her patient. She searched the first aid station's rudimentary supplies doubtfully. The extent and variety of supplies here could definitely be improved upon.

She supposed that as a worst case she could cut the tubing from her stethoscope and use that to make an airway passage. Crazier things had been used, after all, to perform emergency intubations. She set to work—it was clearly going to be a long night.

The long night had passed through dawn and rolled toward noon before Dash stepped out of the compartment. She looked back as she gently closed the door. Both mother and baby daughter were sleeping, and the husband fidgeted in a simple metal chair next to them.

Dash's eyes burned from concentrating for so long. Closing her eyes and not focusing on anything felt luxuriously comfortable. She blinked slowly and thought about going back to her cabin, but she was too enervated to sleep. She realized they must be getting close to their destination. The BrainTrust, and her new lab with the latest modern equipment. With renewed eagerness, she went toward the bow to see if she could spot it yet.

Her first sight of the BrainTrust was obscured by the movements of her two best friends as they flowed through a series of katas. The exercise started slowly at first, but grew ever faster until Dash grew worried she would have to patch one of them up. At first glance, the two fighters seemed terribly mismatched. Jam, significantly taller than her opponent, had the muscular build of an athlete. It looked like she could easily break her thin, even fragile, opponent into little pieces. Ping had clearly been constructed from matchsticks. She was barely taller than Dash herself—the good doctor being perhaps the shortest person on the ferry—but the blurred speed of Ping's relentless attacks put her in contention for the title of "Most Dangerous Person Aboard."

After Dash twisted from side to side a couple of times to try to see past them, she threw up her hands. "Stop it, you two," she demanded as she marched confidently through the middle of the mock combat. She felt a twinge of near-panic as she did so; it was very un-Balinese to interrupt them like this; but she had picked up some very bad habits while studying as an exchange student at Baylor College in Texas.

"Hey, girlfriend!" Jam had a melodious lilt to her voice. She always sounded like she was going to break into song; even her most mundane pronouncements made one want to tap a finger in time with the rhythm.

Ping blew her black hair away from her face. It was an affectation, since the tips of her short bob, which curled toward the edges of her mouth, couldn't actually whip around far enough to get in her way. "Can't you see we're busy here?" Ping's voice, in contrast to Jam's, sounded like a mosquito homing in on its target.

Dash barely heard them as she struggled against the wind. She realized that she faced the ocean's version of Zeno's paradox: with each step she took closer to the rail, the gale grew stronger and made her next step shorter. In the end, she broke the paradox and reached the bow. Holding on for dear life with one hand, she pointed with the other. A short blast of salt spray struck her face, and she turned her head back to her friends. "You two are not doing anything important, and I can see our destination. Have you looked yet?"

"Ooh," Jam and Ping cried in unison. They pushed through the wind to join her. Several tall gleaming ships, mostly white, towered above the sea on the horizon.

"It's not very impressive from here." Dash projected her voice against the wind with a note of disappointment and apology in her voice. In retrospect, she realized that was not surprising. "As large as the cruise liners are—technically they are isle ships, to be more correct--they are too far away for us to appreciate them." She motioned. "Can you make out that black dot next to the second one to the right from the center? That is a ferry like ours." Dash heard both women gasp softly.

Ping squinted as she moved her lips silently. "I count seven of them."

"And maybe another one that looks half-built," added Jam.

"Yes, that would be one of the isle ships they have under construction", Dash explained. "There are currently fourteen full-sized isle ships comprising the BrainTrust mobile archipelago. The other ships will be connected to two new mobile archipelagos. One will take station near the coast of China, and the other will go to the Gulf of Guinea, outside Nigeria."

A thoughtful expression crossed Ping's face. "The Gulf outside Nigeria?" Ping clapped her hands. "Aren't there pirates there? Ooh, I'd *love* to fight pirates!" Ping rubbed her arms. She wore a light sweater on the open deck; Dash knew that beneath the sweater Ping was adorned with two fierce works of art. A tattoo of a blue-green dragon coiled around her upper right arm, its head rising to her shoulder to breathe a jet of orange fire along her collarbone. And upon her left arm a cardinal-red phoenix, long and thin, rose from its ashes, stronger than before.

Jam snorted. "Pirates! You might want to see how you like being a peacekeeper aboard the BrainTrust first. You should at least try your new job before rushing off to the next one." She lightly rubbed the thickened skin of a rough scar beneath her right eye that Dash presumed she'd gotten in the Pakistani Army. "Fighting is not always fun, you know."

Dash answered Ping's earlier question. "Yes, pirates have worked the Gulf of Guinea for decades. In our parents' time Somalia on the east coast of Africa was famous for pirates, of course. But the countries of Nigeria and Benin on the west coast habitually experience the kind of chaos and poverty that encourages such violence. Regardless, I believe the plan is not so much to fight pirates —though I imagine they will do some of that—as to find the best and brightest young minds that currently have little future. The BrainTrust will offer them an immersive education and contract them to become engineers and entrepreneurs. Perhaps a couple of them will even become medical researchers like myself."

The BrainTrust, Dash had come to realize as she read about it, was a mining company. They mined the world for humanity's finest and most underutilized creative minds.

Ping stared at her. "How do you know all that?"

Jam answered, "Because Dash read the website, silly." She smiled. "You and I don't have to read anything, because she'll tell us."

Ping giggled. "We have our own BrainTrust super-genius right here." She poked Dash painfully in the shoulder.

Dash rolled her eyes. She knew better than to rub her sore shoulder; it would only encourage Ping. She pointed again. "There is one of the hydrogen fuel dirigibles. See how it rises as it fills?"

Ping pointed off into the even greater distance. "Is that another one way out there?"

Dash tried to follow Ping's finger. She pushed her glasses higher on her nose, but it did not help; the salt spray clung to the glasses, ruining her ability to see. "You have good eyes. It might be another fuel ship on its way back to deliver its load to San Francisco, but it might also be a GPlex wifi relay balloon. I can't tell from here."

Ping got a faraway look in her eyes. "I'd still like to go to Nigeria," she muttered. "I mean, the BrainTrust is full of geeks and nerds. What are we going to be doing besides escorting tipsy twenty-somethings who are barely able to stand after celebrating their startup's IPO back to their cabins? Being a peacekeeper is going to be *sooo* boring."

The first meeting of the Voice of the Silent was about to be held at Jerry's Auto Repair. Drew sauntered into the shop just in time to watch Jerry stare down at his new bot. The bot methodically droned a dead vehicle's statistics. "Damned robots," Jerry muttered, kicking the machine out of his way. "If they had souls, they'd burn in Hell."

Drew could already see how the first meeting of the Voice was going to go. "Whoa, Jerry! I thought we were saving the Lake of Fire for the damned doctors." He looked at the bot with puzzlement. "Aren't those illegal?"

Jerry tore his gaze away from the bot to focus on Drew. "Nah. It doesn't have hands, see?" The bright safety-orange bot was about the size of a child's red wagon. "Only the general-purpose bots are illegal. This one's only good for diagnostics, inspections, and carrying tools. The man it works for has to do all the serious stuff." He glared at the bot again. "'Course the gov still taxes you an arm and a leg for the damned thing. And it still costs jobs." He rubbed his temples with his right hand. "Even with the taxes, the guys down the street were undercutting me. I had to let Keith go and get this instead just to match their price."

A voice echoed through the garage. Drew could see the silhouette of a tall, thin man haloed by the bright sun at the main door. He had a holstered gun on his hip, which Drew knew was a Colt .45.

Jerry waved. "Howie, come on in."

Howie came in, followed quickly by another tall man with a slight paunch under his striped shirt.

Jerry waved again. "Chuck, good to see you too." He gestured to the back of the shop, where Drew saw a handful of folding chairs arranged in a rough circle. He plopped down in one before the others got there.

Jerry had organized the Voice of the Silent just a month earlier; Chuck, Howie, Drew himself, and Jerry were its only members. But Drew was sure they'd grow once they pulled off their first mission. Their cause was just.

Jerry sat in the chair that was a little separate from the others. "I've got great news, guys! I know what our first target will be. But first, let us pray." He bowed his head, as did Drew and the others, and led the prayer. "Our Father who art in heaven, hallowed be thy name. Give us the strength to oppose the wicked who oppose righteousness. Give us the wisdom to discern friend from foe. Grant us the opportunity to prove our devotion, and if our death should be what is necessary, let your will be done at any price. Amen."

After the last amen, Jerry led everyone to the cooler to grab a beer, and sat down again.

Howie asked the obvious question. "So, Jerry, where're we goin'? Who's lined up in our scope?"

Jerry leaned back in his chair. "We're going to hit the med ship in the BrainTrust. The *Chiron*, it's called."

There was a stunned silence for a moment. Drew spoke for all of them when he said, "That's a mighty long way to go for a first target. I'd sorta expected we'd hit something a little closer, like a clinic in Southern California." Southern California was about as close as you could get to Lodi,

Texas and find a place where the sinners performed abortions. The Red states had destroyed all the abortion clinics years earlier, by the simple expedient of hounding them with hospital-level regulations. By the time an abortion clinic managed to accommodate the regulatory burdens of a hospital, it was far too expensive for it to continue to operate.

Jerry waved the objection away. "I know, I know, you expected us to hit the clinic in Needles, but that's not where our womenfolk go for abortions. The clinics in California are even more expensive than ours if you're out of state, and you have to be a resident for five years to get the free in-state healthcare." He guffawed. "Besides, you know the old joke about healthcare in the Blue states: it may be free, but the waiting line is so long you have to schedule an abortion ten months in advance."

Drew thought it was kind of a dumb joke, but he laughed along with everyone else.

Jerry continued, "No, when our women want an abortion, they go all the way to the BrainTrust. Once you get to San Francisco it's quick and easy: you take the day ferry out to the ships at seven in the morning, they work on you before lunch using the damned surgical robots that aren't certified here so it's real cheap, and take the ferry back that evening. Maybe the boyfriend buys her a nice dinner before leaving, if he's along in the first place." He shook his head. "The lengths evil people will go."

Chuck spoke for the first time. He didn't speak often, but when he did, it was always smart to listen. "Jerry, that all sounds good, but those isle ships in the Brain Trust are all wired with so many video cams they're like holes in a prairie dog town. You can't move an inch without getting recorded."

Jerry leaned forward. "You're too right, Chuck. I don't think there's a chance in hell we won't get caught, but that's where the good news starts. The BrainTrust doesn't have jails or anything—they just send criminals back to the state or country they came from. Now, if they dumped us in California or Oregon and we got tried there, we'd be in trouble. But we're Texas residents, boys. They'll have to send us back here for the trial. I know; I checked." He smiled. "And I think we all know how that'll go."

Everybody else sat back in their chairs and smiled with Jerry. The discussion turned to details of the plan.

2

SIGHTS TO SEE

Cardwell's Law: *Over time, entrenched interests destroy innovation.*

Everyone from the ferry, minus the new mother and her newborn daughter, was escorted to the auditorium. Dash, as was her nature, chose to sit in the front row. Ping and Jam muttered about it, but came with her. They had the first three rows to themselves.

A tall man in a dark blue suit stood at the podium. He had silver hair and a face weathered by age. Ping whispered, "Wow, did they get him from a museum?"

"Shush," Dash whispered back. "He looks very distinguished."

"Dinosaurs look *distinguished*. He looks *old*."

The lights dimmed as the first slide of the man's presentation appeared on the screen. "Welcome, everyone.

My name is Colin Wheeler, and this conglomeration of fourteen isle ships is the BrainTrust. The ship hosting this meeting is the *GPlex I*, one of the first ships built by GPlex and FB for the autonomous mobile archipelago we have today." The screen behind him transitioned to the next slide, an image of all four of the original BrainTrust ships, *GPlex I* and *II*, and *FB Alpha* and *Beta*.

"As most of you know, the first BrainTrust ships were built in haste sixteen years ago, just before Deportation Phase II, when the American national government sent the 101st Airborne Division to Silicon Valley to round up and expel all the foreign engineers. GPlex and FB, having seen the writing on the wall a year earlier, had been rushing to complete the first isle ships and get them into international waters two hundred miles offshore so their foreign employees could go there and still be maximally productive. By the time the troops arrived the GPlex and FB headquarters had only half as many people as they had hosted the year before; only American citizens remained. Copters and ferries could easily shuttle back and forth between the BrainTrust and the Valley, so engineering teams could still have frequent face to face meetings. The President—who had not yet been named President-for-Life—sent a Navy frigate to drive the isle ships all the way across the ocean, but it was met by the newly-formed California Coastal Patrol. The California governor had realized that GPlex and FB—along with lots of other companies in the Valley—would move their operations out to the BrainTrust if they had to, and if that were to happen, the subsequent loss of jobs, increase in welfare rolls, and destruction of the tax base would drive the state into bankruptcy." Colin paused.

"The Coastal Patrol would have been quite overmatched by the Navy frigate sent to force the BrainTrust to leave, but the steadfastness of the Patrol was never put to the test. Quite by coincidence a Chinese cruiser showed up, asserting that if the Americans were going to stick their noses into China's business in the South China Sea, it was only fitting for the Chinese to help ensure that the Law of the Sea was enforced in international waters off the coast of the United States as well."

Quiet laughter bubbled around the auditorium, but Ping squirmed in her seat. "Was this before or after World War II?" she whispered. Dash and Jam both glared her into silence.

The history lesson was brief. Colin moved on to the layout of the ships in the archipelago, showing how one could go from any ship to anyplace else in the BrainTrust, especially the cafeterias, the shopping areas, and medical stations. He finished within half an hour. "Good news! Our time is up. As you look around the auditorium, you'll see a number of guides sent by your various employers to take you on customized tours." He gestured around the auditorium at men and women—all much younger than Colin, Dash noticed—who stood with glowing signs. "If each of you looks at your phone, you'll find an email specifying which guide you should join."

Dash, Jam, and Ping looked at their cells. "I don't have an email," Dash muttered.

"Me either!" Ping cried.

"Neither do I," Jam added softly.

"Nor do you need one." Colin smiled as he stepped in front of them. "You're with me."

In the passageway outside the auditorium, a four-seat vehicle awaited them. It reminded Dash of the bumper cars she'd seen in Hong Kong's Disneyland, though this one had no steering wheel. Colin stepped around it and climbed into the far side. "All aboard!" he called. Once everyone was settled, the vehicle glided silently away.

Ping pounded the back of Dash's seat in a quick rhythm. "I guess you never really get to go very fast here, do you?"

"Nope," Colin answered. "These arvees—Archipelago Electric Vehicles—are limited to thirty kilometers per hour, which is plenty for cruising across the isle ships. You can order one from your phone, and you can get from any point on the archipelago to any other point in seven or eight minutes." The arvee whizzed around a corner, utilizing its collision-avoidance system to weave past a green-and-purple bicycle with a nearly-erect rider. Another bicycle, a streamlined triathlon bike in lustrous black-and-red with the rider bent far over the handlebars, surged past them. "There are a lot of people packed in here, but it's a three-dimensional world—the ships are twenty-five decks tall, so a lot of distance is covered by going up and down elevators, as we are about to do now." The arvee entered a huge elevator, large enough to hold four arvees, and they exited a few decks up.

They emerged next to a passage that led outside through automatic doors. A crisp fresh ocean breeze swirled past them and Jam pulled the scarf covering her head tighter. Her scarf, a swirling rainbow of rich pure colors, gleamed in the sunlight.

As their arvee turned left and glided to the stern, the next isle ship along the eastern edge of the rough rectangle of ships came into view around the towering bulk of *GPlex I*. Dash looked up…and up, and up. From here, the ship looked to be as tall as the sky.

Colin coughed. "Before we start the tour, I need to thank you, Dash, for your work on the ferry coming here. Amanda—Dr. Copeland—said you saved a pregnant woman's life. *Despite* Amanda's help, as she tells the story. I guess there was a rare but fatal complication?"

Dash nodded. "Eighty percent fatal."

Ping, sitting behind Dash, punched her shoulder. "Our own super-genius, and she's a life-saving heroine, too."

Dash slid down in the seat to protect her shoulders from additional compliments. She noticed that Colin was shaking with silent laughter. Dash asked, "So you know Dr. Copeland well?"

Colin nodded. "We have worked together for many years."

Dash leaned forward and turned to look him in the eye. "You are not a typical tour guide."

Colin scrunched his eyebrows as he considered his reply. "Well, giving the tour from time to time *is* one of my duties."

Ping was the first to notice the evasion in the answer and deduce the reason. "Oooh, we're special."

This time Jam punched Ping in the shoulder. "We are not special, foolish one. *Dash* is special."

"Of course," Ping acknowledged contritely. "That's what I meant."

Colin cleared his throat. "So, the first things you should all notice are the bots on cleaning duty." He pointed at a couple machines scrubbing the endless line of Plexiglas panels comprising the transparent gunwales that separated them from a multi-story plunge into the sea. The bots looked like oversize breadboxes with insect legs.

The bots toiled ceaselessly. The panels were so transparent they were mostly invisible, except where the bots washed them. "You'll see bots throughout the ship, twenty-four hours a day. They're an important part of how we can maintain so many residents on the ship. Unlike cruise ships that have hundreds of crewmen working to keep things shipshape and provide services, we have a very small crew, many of whom work as wranglers for the bots that do the maintenance." They rolled around a corner to see a large gray structure floating in the distance. The hull of the vessel was barge-like. In that respect it was similar in design to the isle ships, very wide with no real prow, but the superstructure was featureless and dull, an ungainly half-breed of a ship that sat lower in the water than an isle ship with its cruise liner-style superstructure. Colin pointed. "That is the factory and manufacturing research ship *Hephaestus*. That's where we do all our work with hazardous materials."

Dash added, "For example, currently there is a prototype for a new polysilicon factory. Polysilicon is used to make solar cells, but both the hydrogen chloride and the trichlorosilane used in its manufacture are quite toxic. The

BrainTrust's *Hephaestus* would be an excellent place for a polysilicon factory."

Colin looked at her with some surprise. "It's like Dash said. As the regulatory regime dirtside gets ever more rigid, polysilicon plants are shutting down, leaving an opportunity for us."

Dash switched topics. "And of course the *Hephaestus* is probably where you process spent nuclear fuel from America into new fuel for your own reactors."

Colin's eyes widened and his whole upper body stiffened. "The media generally thinks we just repackage the SNF from the mainland and dump it on the ocean floor."

Dash snorted—another un-Balinese habit she'd picked up in Texas. "I am not the media. I can do math." She pointed out at the bots scrubbing the windows. "You use energy profligately. Washing these transparent sidings takes an enormous amount of fresh water, which means an enormous amount of power." She pointed at the towering bulkheads beside them. "The newest isle ships have superstructures built primarily with magnesium alloys rather than steel. You import no magnesium, therefore, you are extracting it from the ocean. I cannot even imagine how much energy that requires, even if you have a more efficient process than the known state of the art."

Colin was back to laughing silently. "Well, our nuclear reactors are not much of a secret any more anyway. We never actually lied about them, you know. It was just never very politic to mention them in public circles. We let people believe the solar panels and wind turbines on the top decks of *Gplex II* and *FB Beta* supplied our power, if they wanted to believe it." He sighed. "An outraged media storm about our horrific and evil power generation systems has been inevitable for a while now."

Dash asked, "When can I see them? The nuclear reactors, I mean."

Colin considered the question. "Soon."

Ping whispered to Jam in a loud voice, "Did our Dash just score one on the old guy?"

Jam nodded. "I believe so."

The arvee swerved around the outer edge of the last isle ship in the row, allowing them to look north for the first time.

Jam pointed to a new sight in the distance. There were several ships, but their courses looked odd. "It looks like two of those ships are going to crash."

Dash pushed her glasses up her nose; Colin squinted and chuckled. "That's the fishermen and the Greens playing chicken."

Ping observed, "I like playing chicken." Her eyes gleamed. "I always win."

Colin explained. "The Greens want to prevent that cargo ship from coming through the reef to deliver supplies. You can sort of make out our artificial reef, low and dark green; it completely encircles the BrainTrust except for a couple of shipping channels. The merchant ship is heading for one of those channels. The Greens hope to embargo enough deliveries to make the BrainTrust operationally impractical." He pointed toward a ship moving to prevent the Greens from blocking the merchant ship. "But we have a deal with some of the California fishermen. They rent our harvester bots to load up with our kahala from the reef, then they take the haul back to the States. Since the bots are ours, are arguably in international waters, and are not aboard the fishing vessels when they return to port, it is not illegal for the fishing vessels to utilize the bots. And since the fish were caught by American vessels, the fish are not subject to the thirty-five percent import tax. So the fishermen want us to stay, maintain the reef, grow the fish, and rent them the bots. The Greens and the fishermen inevitably butt heads from time to time."

Dash frowned, "I'm surprised the Greens don't just bring a boat into the passage and dump it there."

Colin nodded. "They tried that." He pointed farther to the west. "Do you see the lump in the reef out there?"

The ladies squinted across the water.

"The passage through the reef used to be there. The Greens plugged it with a ship, so we opened the passage you see now and grew the reef into the Green ship, embedding it. Now it's part of the reef." He paused, then continued dryly, "It has become quite a popular tourist attraction."

Ping laughed. "So the Greens enhanced your business. I love using the enemy against himself." She laughed again. "Though that is more Jam's style than mine. I personally prefer to punch people." She tried to hit Jam in the shoulder, but Jam swung her arm in a casual block and deflected the blow into the seat behind her. "Ow!" Ping exclaimed. "See what I mean?"

More silent laughter from Colin. Dash thought he

might be enjoying himself too much. He said, "We have plenty of opportunities to use the strength of our enemies. *Too* many opportunities, actually. Everyone hates us."

Dash gave him a skeptical look. "Surely that is an exaggeration. The fishermen like you, apparently."

"Some fishermen," Colin acknowledged, "but most don't. The shrimpers in the Gulf of Mexico hate us because we farm and export shrimp, and since the shrimpers are from a Red state, the President has banned our shrimp outright. So we export our shrimp to Canada and Australia. The lobstermen in Maine hate us since we also farm lobster. But Maine is a Blue state, so the President allows us to ship lobster tax-free to the States."

The little arvee had been carrying them from ship to ship around the archipelago across tunnel-like gangways with Plexiglas arches. They came around the northwest corner and could see the first hints of the ship in the southwest corner. The superstructure, instead of being white, was a wild swirl of richly saturated colors.

Ping bounced up and down in her seat, rocking the arvee. "I've been meaning to ask about the ship with all the colors. It's beautiful!"

Dash spoke before Colin could answer. "That is the *Elysian Fields*, also known as 'the party boat.' When tourists visit, they stay there. The *Elysian Fields* has all kinds of entertainment, from roulette wheels to twenty-deck-high water slides." She paused. Colin tried to speak, but Dash continued. "Whereas the first BrainTrust isle ships had steel superstructures, the newest ones are made with titanium-coated magnesium. They create the colors by stressing the titanium, as is done for titanium jewelry."

They continued around the party boat and turned the corner to head east. Colin pointed southeast, beyond the low outline of the reef. A long, lean ship cruised slowly, shadowed by a pair of tiny vessels. The little ships looked like a pair of mice attempting to herd a cat. "The California Coastal Patrol gets into it with the US Navy from time to time. Each organization keeps a ship or two out here to protect their interests. Depending on the day of the week, one or the other of them hates us. The Blue unions as well as the Reds who run the federal government hate us for using general-purpose robots to replace human labor. Blues in general hate us for supplying a handy high-tech tax haven, but currently the California Blues like us because we send them hydrogen-filled dirigibles from which they pump the hydrogen and burn it so San Francisco can have both nighttime electricity and drinking water."

Dash muttered, "I have wondered about that. Big as the dirigibles are, do they really supply enough hydrogen fuel to make a difference?"

Colin shrugged. "Every little bit of water you can produce helps when you're in the seventh year of a five-year drought. And every little bit of energy you can generate after midnight helps when the dependency of your grid on wind and solar is so high that nighttime power production falls so low you have regular pre-dawn brownouts. The brownouts are the reason GPlex planted a third isle ship out here stuffed with nothing but servers a few years back. They needed reliable power. They considered putting a server farm in Tennessee, where they still burn coal all night for power, but the federal law requiring full continuous government surveillance of all data is rigidly enforced in the Red states. We won the bid."

He went back to listing his litany of haters. "The Red states and Federal government in America may have the most complicated relationship with us. Religious conservatives hate that we offer low-cost abortions to medical tourists. Electric utilities like us because we take some of their spent nuclear fuel. The NSA hates us because we manufacture computer chips that don't have back doors built in, making them harder to hack. The CIA likes us because they buy our chips for their own computers so they can't be easily hacked. Farmers and ranchers like us because we import wheat and beef. Doctors hate us for stealing their patients, for using AI for some of the diagnosis/prescription tasks, and for using robots for surgeries. Lawyers hate us for using only binding arbitration to settle disputes, especially the medical disputes that are so lucrative dirtside."

He took a breath. "Again, depending on which day of the week it is, the Federal government considers our reef to be either a navigation hazard to be destroyed or, since we're currently only fifty miles offshore to deliver hydrogen to California more easily, they consider this reef to be part of the Exclusive Economic Zone for the USA, so it's theirs to fish as they wish. The third legal interpretation is, of course, that it is ours, since we built it and maintain it beyond American territorial waters, but that is never their interpretation."

Dash spoke as he paused. "I still do not see why the Greens dislike you."

"Ah, yes, the Greens. Well, as I said, one of our businesses is collecting spent nuclear fuel, which the Nuclear Regulatory Commission pays us to dispose of. The Greens see this as a problem because it weakens the arguments against the nuke plants, which the Greens want closed at all costs. And of course there's the fact that we built two artificial reefs, one here outside the contiguous zone limit and another where we often anchor, two-hundred miles out on the high seas. Alas, the reefs are…ahem…artificial. So they want to destroy the reefs, but the fish and plants that grow because of the reef are natural and must be protected. And of course the BrainTrust ships are an abomination no matter what, a polluting stain on the ocean."

Dash shook her head. "But you're in the middle of the San Francisco Oceanic Dead Zone, where all the oxygen has been consumed by algal blooms driven by phosphates dumped into the ocean by the city. This BrainTrust reef we see here is the only place in a hundred kilometers where one can find a diversity of ocean life."

"Not as much diversity as the Greens would like, since we harvest the algae and fish we want and cull the ones we don't."

Dash continued her thought, "And the BrainTrust is actually a carbon sink, pulling as much carbon out of the air as a city like Cupertino releases."

"You've been reading our website. We sell the carbon credits in Europe, but the Greens still consider us a pox upon the water."

"I suppose the Greens will get angrier as they come to fully realize that your entire fleet is powered by nuclear reactors."

Colin nodded his head. "Very likely indeed."

In the beginning, the most radical Green group was Earth First!. They were ineffectual; a more determined commitment was required to drive so important a movement. Thus, a number of members formed the more serious Earth Liberation Front. To no avail; the seas continued to rise and the forests continued to wither. A truly dedicated, considerably more violent group splintered from them to become the Earth Liberation Crusade. The ELC had pursued the protection of the Earth with commitment and high explosives, but their urgently necessary success still lay in the future.

The Emeryville chapter of the ELC was referred to rather derisively by the leadership in Berkeley as the Peter, Paul, and Mary chapter. Peter, the founder of the chapter, had not understood the reference when he first heard it, but after he looked it up he was furious. His group was not some gaggle of Sixties folk singers; they were a serious action team.

Peter confessed to himself that the nickname had produced a positive effect: it had given him the angry drive needed to embrace this next operation. They were going to go big.

At this moment, however, his anger was a little subdued. Peter, Paul, and Mary had fallen on hard times. It was hard to light the fuse of worldwide revolution when you were shivering. Peter pulled his sweater tighter around himself and swallowed a curse. *He was sitting in his own living room, dammit.* How could his own living room be this cold? But the outside night was nippy, and the electricity was out again. "I can't believe it! They've been using nukes all these years and we never knew."

Justin, the team member who had been entirely forgotten by the rest of the movement because he didn't even rate a place in the group's nickname, was the pastiest-skinned and nerdiest of the four of them. He complained, "Well, some of us were pretty sure they were using nukes, but you guys—almost everyone in the movement—bought the idea that they were using solar and wind since they had turbines and panels on top of two of the first ships." He plucked at his "Cherish the Earth or Perish with It" t-shirt. He was overweight, unlike the others in this tight circle of friends, and alone among them, he always felt warm. "Then when people started to notice that the BrainTrust's power never went out even after days and days of clouds without much wind, people said, 'Oh, they must be using OTEC!'" (Ocean Thermal Energy Conversion power plants had been all the rage for a while in some Green circles.) "But I always knew that was bullshit, because they move their damn ships around. OTEC is really hard to move—it's even harder to move than those isle ships—and you'd need a freakin' shitload of 'em to make as much power as they use."

Mary, wearing her signature "Green is Life; Gray is Death" t-shirt, shouted in a squeaky voice, "It's an abomination! I always said it was an abomination!"

Paul, whose t-shirt advised, "Conserve the Earth, We Only Have One," put his hand on Mary's shoulder. "And you were always right, Mary, and we always agreed. We just didn't agree enough to get violent about it."

Mary jumped up. "We have to do something!"

Peter rose slowly to his feet and made a calming motion. His sweater loosened, making the "Think Big!" slogan on the t-shirt underneath visible. "And we *will* do something, Mary, but not tonight. Tonight we have to plan."

Justin lifted an eyebrow. "Plan? What are we planning?"

Peter answered grimly. "We're going to knock out one of those nukes. We're gonna turn that whole repugnant fleet into a radioactive wasteland like the West Coast Waste and the North Waste."

Justin looked stunned, then scared, and then, slowly, excited. "The West Waste and the North Waste were created by nuclear missiles. We can show the world that nuclear power plants are like missiles, just waiting to go off." He wiped sweat from his upper lip. "I like it."

Pleading another meeting, Colin directed the arvee to stop and let him off at the *GPlex I*. Before he debarked he instructed the arvee to deliver Dash, Jam, and Ping to their new homes on board the *Chiron*, the ship specializing in medical research and tourism. As he gave the arvee the directions, they learned that Jam and Ping would share a cabin adjacent to Dash's, just as they had on the ferry.

Dash was delighted. "That's marvelous!"

Ping was similarly pleased. "What a magnificent coincidence."

Colin shrugged. "Not really a coincidence. Cabins are generally allotted in sequence as they become available and people arrive. If you look at the distribution of departures and arrivals, it's not unheard of for people arriving on the same ferry to wind up co-located."

Jam spoke next, more slowly. "But only if the people from the ferry also happen to be assigned to the same ship."

Colin nodded. "True. Dash was, of course, always destined for *Chiron*, since that's where her lab is and we like to put people's homes close to their work. You two, as security guards, could have wound up anywhere." He thought about it for a moment. "We have fourteen ships, but not all of them have the same number of security guards. You probably had one chance in ten of being assigned here." Colin stepped away from the arvee and waved as they left.

The trip only took a couple of minutes.

Every deck of every ship had a different outdoor theme for artwork and decorations. The themes varied from whimsical, such as Dundee Outback, to majestic, as with Montana Sky. Colin had explained that the theming had started on *Elysian Fields* so that inebriated tourists could tell if they were on the right deck. The BrainTrust's designers had taken the theme idea from a book, **A Pattern Language**, that Colin had mentioned so reverently Dash made a note to look it up sometime. The decorating on *Elysian Fields* had gotten so much praise that the owner/operators of many of the other isle ships got into a bit of a competition for the best and most beautiful deck themes.

Dash, Jam, and Ping were quartered on the Appalachian

Spring deck. The passage bulkheads were covered in photorealistic murals of the iconic eastern American mountains. A depiction of a stand of lush red and pink rhododendron bushes, so detailed it seemed you could touch them, stood higher than their heads between the doors to their cabins.

Two large suitcases sat in front of Dash's entry, and half a dozen crates sat beside Ping and Jam's door. Dash watched an arvan, a self-driving cargo carrier slightly longer than their arvee, whisk itself away. She muttered. "I guess the van dropped off our stuff." She thumbed open her door and clumsily heaved the first suitcase inside. When she returned, she was limping.

Jam noticed the limp. "Are you okay?"

Dash lifted the second suitcase upright. "Yes. I am missing much of the cartilage in my left knee. It does not bother me unless I try to run or—" she heaved again "carry heavy objects." She finished moving the suitcase with a jerk before Jam could offer to help, and suggested, "Shall we get something to eat in maybe half an hour?" Gaining acknowledgment from her friends, she closed her door to unpack.

Ping looked at Jam. "These are all my crates," Ping said. "Did they lose your luggage someplace?"

Jam shook her head. "For me, the BrainTrust is a new beginning." She held up the shoulder pack she'd carried with her on the ferry. "This is all I have."

Ping looked a little sad. Her expression became apologetic, but then it changed to joy. "Great! I can use a whole wall for my display!"

Jam gave her a sideways glance. "Display of what?

Weapons? Hand-to-hand, of course—swords, maces, that sort of thing?"

Ping laughed. "How'd you know?"

Jam grabbed one of Ping's crates and carried it over the threshold into the bare cabin. "If I can focus your attention for just a couple of minutes, we need to have a serious discussion."

Ping studied her in surprise. "No! I refuse to believe it!"

"If you read between the lines of Mr. Wheeler's calculations, there was one chance in ten that *one* of us would wind up on the *Chiron* with Dash. The chances that both of us would wind up next to Dash were less than one in a hundred. Someone put us near her on purpose."

"You're kidding!" Suddenly Ping's expression changed. Where Ping had stood one moment, an owlish analyst stood the next. Her voice lowered a full octave. "I figured that out when they threw out my perfectly fine roommate to put you in with me, then went out of their way to make sure that both of us—both peacekeepers with mad skills—got to know our super-genius friend."

"Someone's afraid for her," Jam said to this surprising new person.

"They certainly are."

"Someone who knows something we don't."

"So we'll take turns making sure she's covered."

Jam looked pensively at her roommate. "I thought it would be more difficult to get your participation."

"We'll take care of her, Jam." Then Ping's expression changed back to "wild-eyed child," as if the sober analyst was a facade she could only hold for a few moments before reverting to her natural state. "Even if nothing else goes wrong, Dash is very attractive. She's bound to wind up with a bad boyfriend or two. When we find out, we'll discourage them—beat them black and blue, or break their legs." She brightened even more, and her voice rose to its normal pitch. "Or, as a last line of defense, we'll sleep with them!"

Jam grabbed another crate and carried it in. "I guess that's a plan," she agreed doubtfully.

3

FIRST COINS IN THE FOUNTAIN

To find something better you have to try something new.
—Joe Quirk and Patri Friedman, *SeaSteading*

"Dr. Ambarawati, you may go in now." The admin smiled and nodded toward the door.

Dash entered the inner sanctum of the Director of Research for the *Chiron* isle ship. The white-haired woman she had seen on the screen in the middle of her emergency childbirth procedure rose from her desk and came around it to greet her. Dash spoke first. "Dr. Copeland, nice to meet you in person."

"Hopefully we won't get disconnected this time," Amanda Copeland said as they shook hands. Dr. Copeland pointed Dash to a chair on one side of a small mahogany table while taking the chair on the adjacent side. The screen embedded in the table lit up, showing the terms of a contract. "Call me Amanda, please" she continued.

"And I am Dash."

A soft smile lit Amanda's face. "So I'm told." She turned serious. "I need to make sure you understand the contract. You'll be working halftime as a surgeon for normal patients who come to the BrainTrust as medical tourists, and halftime on your telomere research."

"I read the contract quite carefully," Dash confirmed.

"Good. Let's skip to the cool part that isn't in the contract."

Dash raised an eyebrow.

"One of the reasons your research proposal was reviewed more favorably here than anywhere else is that we have a prototype machine that should be able to accelerate your work. It uses techniques derived from CRISPR to build viral factories that manufacture nonreplicating pseudoviruses, which in turn implement a molecular splicing process of one's own design. Of course, none of the literature we publish refers to it as a virus builder—bad press, you know. We call our machine the CRISPIER." She chuckled. "With proper programming, it should be able to produce your telomere manipulators. It's all quite safe. The factories replicate in concentrated hydrogen peroxide, then you add the ingredients for your pseudovirus, and they start producing. Neither the factories nor their products can reproduce outside the peroxide bath. You extract your products from the solution and inject them into the bloodstream, where they then start performing the function you've specified in their design." She tapped the tabletop screen, brought up a picture of the CRISPIER, and gave Dash a brief description of what it could do.

Dash's eyes widened. "This is extraordinary." Her face wore a contemplative smile as she considered the consequences. "If I understand correctly, I could start human trials almost immediately, if I were able to design the factories easily."

Amanda gave her a smug look. "I think you'll find designing pretty straightforward. I already have your intern working on it —Byron Schultz, you'll meet him later today." She looked away, not quite blushing. "The CRISPIER is my own project, so I couldn't help getting started a little bit ahead of time."

Dash laughed. "An ulterior motive. I can see why you accepted my proposal and invited me here."

Amanda pursed her lips and answered slowly, "I'm happy to have you here working with my own research, but I need to be honest. When the Board reviewed your proposal, I voted against inviting you."

Dash's expression shifted to surprise.

"Dash, I'm not sure the world is ready for your work. To oversimplify—to put it the way the press will spin it when word gets out—you're about to invent the Fountain of Youth."

Dash giggled briefly, then stopped; she hated it when she giggled. "It most certainly is not a Fountain of Youth, *Bu* Amanda." She shook her head. "Even if we could repair the telomere chains perfectly and the cells began dividing and replacing themselves with renewed versions, we still would have to devise a way to fix the aging mitochondria to give people the energy they had in their youth. And a host of other problems would need to be fixed as well."

Amanda sat back and waved her hand. "Yes, yes, you're very careful with your claims. You're a very good researcher: ever so cautious, no assertion without a thousand detailed caveats. But make no mistake, the proverbial Fountain lies at the end of the path you're walking."

"If you are opposed to my research, why am I here?"

Amanda turned her head and gazed out the window at the bright blue sea as she remembered her first conversation about Dash, her hopes, and her dreams.

———

She had been sitting in this same office at this same table. Amanda had had her thumbs pressed into her temples, her eyes closed. "Why are you so nuts about this girl, Colin?"

Colin spoke softly. "She's a polymath, Amanda, a full-fledged, full-blooded polymath. You saw the resume."

"I saw the list of things she's interested in. But just because she's interested in all those things doesn't mean she can make contributions in any of those fields. Every grad student in our history has presented a plateful of different kinds of research he wanted to do. We always have to force them to pick one thing, one thing only, and do it well. You know that. Dyah is a medical specialist, not a polymath."

Colin laughed. "You haven't looked closely at the list of publications she put at the end. Did you see the note she had written for improving the neutronics in molten salt nuclear reactors? Or the questions she asked leading to a proposal for a better sintering process for 3D printers?" He snorted. "She was a surgeon by day. She worked on telomeres by night. She worked in a hospital with no research facilities to speak of, and still she made progress. You understand how remarkable that is?" He sighed, then gave her a wicked smile. "You have the resume there? Let me show you a link you may not have read." He borrowed her tablet and flipped pages. "Read."

Amanda started reading. At first she was puzzled, but then her eyes widened. "She's...she's reinventing my own gene splicer."

Colin laughed. "Yes! And that is why I want her here." He paused. "Polymaths—there are so few of them, Amanda. Anybody with a top-range intellect dirtside gets browbeaten into a specialty. You know that, you've seen it even with our first investors. It's hardly better on the Brain-Trust, right here in your own research complex. Heck, you just admitted you're part of the problem."

Amanda drew herself up. "Colin, I don't drive anyone to be a one-trick pony. I just want them to focus on one thing long enough to get their degree. Once their degree is done, if they stop expanding their horizons and just continue to do what they've been doing, that's their choice. Don't blame me for this."

Colin waved his hand. "Ancient battles, with people who aren't even alive any more. Sorry I got sidetracked."

"Don't try to fool me on this. If you want her here just because she's a polymath, bring her in to work on our reactors. But not telomeres, Colin! If you let her work on telomeres, she'll become the nexus of the crisis—the crisis we've been dodging for sixteen years now—very successfully I might add, and all because of you, if I can say that without swelling your idiot head beyond recognition. Why are you dead-set on kicking off the crisis now? We still aren't strong enough to fight them all."

Colin's gaze went to the window and he looked into the clear, unbound sky. "I won't deny I wouldn't mind waiting another ten years while they got weaker and we got stronger, but... Amanda, Dyah is going to bring on the crisis whether we help her or not. She's going to pursue her goal, and she's going to succeed. If she's here, we have a better chance of bringing everyone safely through. And by 'everyone,' I mean everyone including Dyah herself. Her research will get her killed, though I doubt she understands that." He shook his head. "The balance is about to shift. That's not a question any longer. When it shifts, we need to be able to choose the direction we'll leap as we fall." He smiled. "Besides, I have a plan."

Amanda growled, "We aren't your puppets, Colin."

Colin's smile turned sour. "You think I don't know that? Does anyone ever let me forget it for even one minute?"

Amanda shook her head, returning to the present. Apparently reminiscing had not taken too long, because Dash was not looking at her like she was having a seizure just yet. "Have you given any thought to who your first patients will be?"

Dash nodded. "A little. Obviously they will be quite old, preferably with no special ailments. And since the therapy will be quite expensive at first, I expect they will be wealthy."

"Will they be powerful?"

Dash looked at her in puzzlement.

Amanda reached over and touched her hand. "The world's aging and decrepit dictators will be first in line, my dear unpolitical friend. Some of them will not take no for an answer."

Dash shook her head emphatically. "It's still experimental. In the first trials it will be at least as likely to kill them as increase the ability of their aging cells to divide and create fresh replacements."

"Those who are near death anyway will not care."

Dash frowned. "Then they are fools. This is not the Fountain of Youth—it's just telomeres."

He sat in the big chair with his feet on the desk. It was always calming for him to sit here, looking around the curves of the room and seeing the bright powerful seal on the floor. When you thought about it, the room was impractical. You couldn't really use the space in an oval room efficiently. Where did you put the stuff that should have gone in the corners?

But the room and its symbols of power were not sufficiently calming today. As he listened to the disagreeable voice at the other end of the phone, he lifted his legs off the desk and slammed his feet down on the floor. It was a futile gesture. The plush carpet silently soaked up the impact.

How could he, the most powerful man on earth, be denied?

The Chief Advisor gripped his cell phone like he was about to throw it across the room and repeated his main point. "I'm making this request on behalf of the President-for-Life of the most important country in the world! This is an opportunity to receive your doctor as an honored guest and allow her to perform her therapy on the President himself! I should be met with a 'Yes, *sir*, thank you, *sir*!' I should *not* be greeted with a traitorous 'No!' You're still a United States citizen, let me remind you, and this is treason!"

The voice on the phone seemed quite unaffected by his rant. It was as if the speaker were himself so formidable that he could talk down to the most powerful man in the world...which, the Advisor had to acknowledge, was not as crazy as it sounded. Sure, the guy was stuck on a defense-less slug of a ship, but despite being defenseless, the speaker controlled a significant asset. Very significant—at least as significant as owning a country. And that asset was the one thing, as it happened, that the Advisor needed rather desperately.

The voice spoke. "You're accusing me of treason? Isn't that the black hole calling the kettle dark?" The Advisor spluttered as the voice continued, "But let us not get side-tracked. I'm perfectly happy to let you talk to her and let her make up her own mind."

The Advisor smiled. It lasted only a moment before the voice spoke again. "Before she commits, however, I am optimistic that she will let me highlight a few points for her."

The Advisor closed his eyes.

"Let me be certain I understand the honor being bestowed here. She is to be flown to the Capital secretly, she is to set up her facility in a secret wing of Walter Reed Hospital, she is to rejuvenate the President-for-Life in secret, and then, if everything goes as hoped, she will be flown back to us here on the BrainTrust, again secretly. Correct?"

"Exactly so," the Advisor agreed.

"Forgive me, Mr. Chief Advisor, but that doesn't sound so much like an honor as a dirty fact no one wants to acknowledge."

"The anonymity is for her own good. I presume she doesn't want to become famous yet."

"Hmmm... Why don't you fly out here with the President and let Dash treat him in her own facility?"

The Advisor glared at the phone. "You know why. We can't have people thinking that America, the most creative society on earth, is dependent for key inventions on...on a little brown girl in your floating sardine can out in the middle of the ocean."

"Ah. The honesty soars as the quality of discourse dives off a cliff. Very good. Publicly welcoming a brilliant Balinese medical research scientist from the BrainTrust to the White House would pop that bubble about American innovation, would it not?"

"It is your duty to your country to assist her to see her way clear to help us," the Advisor ground out.

"There are also a few problems associated with the possibility—the distinct possibility—that things might not turn out as well as projected. It seems unlikely, for example, that her therapy in its current form will shave more than a few years off the President's age. Figure ten, as a best guess. He'd still be biologically eighty years old if the therapy were to be successful."

The Advisor thought about that for a moment. "That's fine. That's almost perfect, in fact." His voice turned humorous. "The last thing we want is for him to get so spry he wants to take back control of his Twitter account."

"Well, it's good to know you don't want to go overboard with this rejuv business," the voice remarked with only the slightest hint of mockery. "But it gets worse. There's a very good chance he'd die. Given the state of Dash's therapy at this time, it's best thought of as a high-tech form of Russian roulette. You do understand that this is a speculative undertaking, right?"

"I'm sure you can improve the odds for the President."

"Mr. Chief Advisor, medical outcomes are not subject to the fake news, alternative facts, or whimsical beliefs of the White House. Here's the thing: if she agrees to come to you, Dr. Ambarawati will be conducting a therapy that has not been certified by the FDA, using equipment that is also not certified by the FDA." The voice paused. "We had a brief conversation with an FDA representative about the equipment, as it happens. He was quite enthusiastic. He gave us seven hundred and fifty three pages of forms to fill out and told us how to spend the first hundred million on certification testing. After the results from the first hundred million came in, the FDA would then have enough information to tell us how to spend the next several hundred million. He told us to take as long as we needed. Very helpful, your FDA was."

The Advisor just grunted. "It's not like the FDA would ever know about the operation."

"Umm... If the President died undergoing an uncertified procedure with uncertified equipment, Dr. Ambarawati would be guilty of murder, would she not?"

The Advisor rolled his eyes. "That's an extremely rigid legal interpretation. The legal system hasn't been allowed to be that inflexible for more than a decade." He cheered up as he realized he finally had an opening to start negotiating. That was all he really needed: a chance to negotiate, give and take, and take and win. He started by making a first offer. "We could put together a document freeing her of responsibility—"

"Which you would deny the moment the people found out the President-for-Life was dead. You'd be on the edge of a civil war. You'd sacrifice the good doctor to win Blue votes in a heartbeat. Heck, your own Reds would demand her head."

"I'd still honor my promise."

"Why would you change policies now?"

"I'd still have control of the government, dammit!"

"Yes, of course. Like I said, a civil war."

The Advisor felt a headache coming on. "When you decide to do your patriotic duty, call my office. My admin will put you through." He hung up on the traitor with a stab of his finger and longed, just for a moment, for the good old days where you could slam the receiver down to vent your feelings. Possibly even throw the phone.

Well, he had suspected he might be snubbed like this. He was tempted to just tell the captain of the cruiser *Vella Gulf*, currently stationed outside the BrainTrust, to lob a few Tomahawk cruise missiles into the place. Strictly as a negotiating tactic, of course. A little softening up. But the Chinese might object, since two Politburo members had children attending the university there. The Russian Union President had a niece there too, if he remembered correctly. And a Red senator and a couple Blue congressmen had kids there as well, let's not forget. Best not to be hasty.

Still, he had the most powerful military force on Earth, and the BrainTrust was the most defenseless target in history. He still had options. Excellent options, even. And this way, once he had the doctor, there would be no reason to give her back. He could use her himself when he needed her some years down the road.

He was still agitated. Some release would be good. "Trixie!" he yelled, "I need you in here now!" She would help him calm down.

Colin put his cell down. "And so the mighty send commands unto us from the heights of Olympus." He shook his head ruefully. "I just wish he hadn't called me from the White House. Now the Russian Union President knows about Dash too." He sighed. "Yet another player enters the game."

Amanda stared at him open-mouthed. "Are you telling me the Russians have the White House bugged?"

Colin waved his hand. "Common knowledge. Everybody but the Chief Advisor knows his admin is a Russian agent."

"I just thought that was Blue fake news."

Colin shook his head. "Not according to my contacts. I still have a few, you know. They keep begging him to replace her, but he insists she couldn't be a Russian spy because the Russians are his friends."

Amanda rolled her eyes. "Great. Can't wait to hear from the Russians next."

Colin frowned. "Oh, I'd love to wait. Alas, I don't think that will be one of our choices."

The President of the Russian Union drummed his fingers on his dark and massive desk. Four people were required to move it, which he did often, just for the pleasure of watching his people work so hard on something so pointless.

So, the BrainTrust had someone working on the Fountain of Youth! And making progress, enough that the Americans were very interested. Desperate, some might say. And for good reason. Unlike himself, the fools had never actually taken full control of the election process. As one of his predecessors had observed, it made no difference who voted, it only mattered who counted the votes. How could the Chief Advisor not understand a lesson that simple?

The Chief Advisor had been a valuable piece on the Russian Union's chess board for many years now. While giving the Advisor the tips he needed to bank the occasional billion dollars, the surveillance bugs in the White House had supplied him with the info he needed to personally make hundreds of billions from various enter-prises. Even better, the Advisor had unwittingly told him just how much of Poland he could grab for the Russian Union before the Americans would get involved, which would have been messy. It had been a great relationship. It would be sad to lose it. There was significant merit to staying out of the way and letting the Chief Advisor snatch the doctor and fix the American President, to keeping things the way they were.

On the other hand, having a doctor who could rejuve-nate him personally was too big an opportunity. The Russian Union President wasn't getting any younger. Sure, he gave people press photos of himself riding horses, playing hockey, and winning at judo, but it was getting harder. He needed rejuvenation almost as much as the American President. He certainly deserved it more.

He would have to move fast, however. The doctor would be much harder to seize once she was locked up in DC. Extracting her from the BrainTrust should be easy.

He really needed to give Trixie a bonus. He had broken her and trained her from a young age to do whatever it took to serve the Motherland, and she had been performing brilliantly ever since he arranged for her to meet the Chief Advisor. He chuckled to himself, thinking about her descriptions of how, after learning a sweep for bugs was coming, she would run around the White House whisking them all away, then replanting them after the sweep was finished. Great stuff. A shame they couldn't write a book about her exploits.

The Chief Advisor probably had her in his office right now. Thinking about that, the President rang for Pascha—

Trixie's sister, who'd had the same training—to join him on the desk.

Dash walked through the austere passages of Deck Twelve, the Red Planet deck, wearing a new lab coat with a new stethoscope draped over it. She had to confess she was not enamored of the Red Planet theme. The passages were lined with unrelenting photorealistic red rock from horizon to horizon, except where the horizon was blocked by mountains and ridges, also riven from unrelenting red rock. Only one spot broke the sense of endless wasteland. As she came out of the passage into a wider area, the rendering granted a distant view of Falcon's Nest, the Mars colony, ensconced in its immense transparent geodesic dome.

She had run into Colin at the ramps that diverged between Decks Eleven, Twelve, and Thirteen. Deck Eleven, she could not help noticing, was lushly green, the jungle forest of Wenara Wana. Also known as Bali's Monkey Forest, Wenara Wana meshed with and spilled into the city of Ubud, where she had long ago practiced medicine. Half in jest, she had asked her former tour guide if there was someone she could talk to about switching the themes of Decks Eleven and Twelve. Not, she explained, just so she could feel more at home in her lab. No, she could not help believing that the greenery would be soothing for her experimental patients, and would help in their recovery. Colin had smiled and promised to see what he could do. Deck Eleven was currently empty for remodeling anyway.

And he had a little pull, he explained, with some of the people in charge.

But for now, she walked through the unyielding immensity of the Red Planet. When she arrived at her new lab she found a college-age kid with thick black hair, pale skin sprinkled with acne, and a sincere, driven expression. He seemed awfully young to her. She had to laugh at herself, looking down from her mature twenty-seven years upon someone no more than seven years younger than she.

Alas, "looking down" was never really an option for her. As usual, she had to look up to meet this new person's eyes. "You Americans are all too tall," she muttered. She smiled and held out her hand. "I'm Dash. I would bet that you are Byron Schultz."

He smiled, but it did not reach his serious dark eyes. "I'm here to assist you any way I can."

"*Bu* Amanda tells me you have already helped me considerably. Thank you." To break the ice, she asked, "How did you wind up here as my intern?"

"Grew up in Portland," he began. Realizing a woman from Bali might not know where that was, he explained. "A bit south of the West Coast Waste."

"Aha. You wanted to help people with radiation poisoning."

He nodded. "At first I figured there might be something one could do with stem cells, so I went to Berkeley and joined the research center there. But…" He drew his hand through his hair, caught it, and pulled, "it costs almost a billion dollars to get a promising stem cell therapy through the certification process these days. Who's going to pay for it? California, Oregon, all the Blue states have terminated most medical research to reduce costs." He dropped his hand, letting it slap lightly against his leg. "It just isn't practical."

"Very disheartening. I see why you came to the Brain-Trust. But why my lab? I am not doing stem cells."

A look of anger fleetingly crossed his face, then he laughed. "Because your research is even bigger and more important. Telomere chains! You can fix all kinds of things, including radiation damage."

Dash held up her hand in a "Stop" gesture. "Only radiation damage that has not compromised the cell's ability to produce a healthy replacement. Do not confuse my research with a universal cure. Many people are apparently making that mistake already. I will not have such a person in my lab." She paused. "Lengthening the telomere chains may even amplify the dangers of radiation, since cancer cell telomere chains don't behave normally. Indeed, if something goes wrong, my therapy may cause whole new types of uncontrollable cancers and tumors."

Byron waved a hand impatiently. "Yes, yes, we are playing with fire." He smiled sheepishly. "I guess that was a reason I wanted to be here, too."

"Excellent. Can you show me what you've been doing with the CRISPIER?"

———

The world was dim and quiet save for the glow of the screens as Byron showed Dash the work he had already done. As they ran the simulation of the viral factory programming, Dash gasped: it ran so much faster than anything she had been able to do back in Bali. It took her a few minutes and several runs to realize that the new speed of her computations demanded a change in the way she worked.

Back home she would very carefully plan a simulation run, taking all evening after she got home from the hospital and then letting the sim run all night. But now, with the sims coming back so fast she could hardly think between submitting the job and seeing the outcome, she realized that meticulously spending hours to craft the next design no longer made sense. She would become a tinkerer instead, making an improvement in the design, running it, seeing how it went wrong, correcting that, and running it again, all in a matter of minutes.

The tools for programming the factories, however, were too clumsy to support the pace of modification she desired. Time and again the modified design, even when created by Byron—who was at this point highly proficient —broke the sim. "I think this can be improved upon," Dash said quietly as she watched such a failure for the fourth time in a row. Byron looked aside from the screens and eyed her quizzically. She sketched out an idea for making the basic factory template more modular, so that errors could not cause surprising side effects far from the location where the modification had been made. Byron nodded seriously and opened another screen; a whole new kind of software code appeared. "Let's fix it," he said with a light in his eyes. "We'll rebuild the tools so we can redesign the factories." With that, Byron dove deep into the structure of tools themselves, leaving Dash behind.

Several minutes passed before he came up for air and

smiled. "You realize that modifying the tools to modify the programs to modify the viruses is unlikely to work the first time." They entered Dash's newest improvement much more simply than they had before, and ran the sim. Despite Byron's warning, the result was much as had been planned.

"Victory! Well done, Byron."

And so they continued, modifying the factories, then modifying the tools to make it easier to modify the factories, again and again. They made some horrible mistakes, but that was ok. Dash understood that human beings, herself included, learned best when making errors.

Meanwhile, this was the first time Dash had ever worked with someone else on her telomere project. She had never known what it could be like. She hoped henceforth to work this way always.

Finally Dash proposed a radical modularization redesign of the basic template, much more radical than the first one. Byron slumped in his chair. "That's a great idea, Dash, but we'll have to modify the CRISPIER's hardware to support it. We'll have to get a couple of Amanda's engineers in here to help us."

Dash shook her head, blinking, as she came out of the near-trance of their intellectual labors. "Well, on the bright side, I am not quite late for lunch. I am scheduled to meet two friends of mine. Would you care to join us?"

He gave her a goofy grin. "Sure."

As they strode down the passage toward the nearest elevator, Dash asked, "How do you like it here on the BrainTrust? I would guess most Americans would find it very cramped, with our cabins so small."

"Oh, I don't mind the small rooms. I don't spend much

time in my room anyway, and my roommate spends even less. The rooms are all about the same size, so it's pretty egalitarian."

Dash had a cabin all to herself, a perk of being a research lead and project owner, she guessed, but he was right. All the cabins were the same size, and to the best of her knowledge, no one had two unless they had children.

Byron continued. "But from a social perspective, the BrainTrust is pretty backward."

Dash shook her head. "What does that even mean?"

"There are almost no rules to protect people from exploitation. There's no minimum wage, for example."

"I see." They stepped off the elevator and Dash looked around at people moving swiftly on their appointed tasks. "What is the minimum wage in your home?"

"Thirty dollars an hour in California, thirty-five in Portland," he answered crisply.

"Does anyone here on the BrainTrust make less than that?"

"Well, no. All the low paying jobs are done by bots, and the bot wranglers make pretty good money."

Dash thought the facts spoke for themselves, but quickly learned that they didn't.

"The wranglers are still being exploited, though. I mean, with ten bots that never rest or tire in the typical swarm, the people are getting fifteen times as much work done as a dirtside worker, but they don't make anywhere near that much money."

"I see, I guess, though many of the people who were my patients back home would be delighted to make as much money as a BrainTrust wrangler. Indeed, they would be happy to make as much money as one of your bots." They entered the cafeteria and saw Ping and Jam. "My friends are over there." After grabbing trays and running through the buffet tables, they joined Dash's friends. Dash took a seat next to Ping and introduced Byron, who sat beside Jam. Dash looked at Ping, who was making a face. "Are you okay?" Dash asked.

Ping answered, "They said this dulse was supposed to taste like bacon. It's terrible." She thrust a flaky leaf of purple something at Jam. "Jam, does this taste like bacon to you?"

Jam delicately took a bite of the dulse. "It is not too bad," she said cautiously, "though I have no idea if it tastes like bacon."

Ping put her hand down. "You've never had bacon?!"

Dash kicked Ping under the table. "Ping," she hissed, "Of course she has never had bacon."

"Oh. Yeah." She picked up another piece of dulse and held it toward Dash.

Dash looked at it dubiously. "As it happens, I have never had bacon, either. Still…" Like Jam, Dash took a small bite. She shook her head. "I suppose I could eat it," she looked down at her plate, "but today I think I shall stick with Shrimp Alfredo."

"*Hmmph*. Well, they say it works best with lettuce and tomato." After reintegrating the dulse into her BLT, Ping took a big bite. "Ok, not bad, though next time I'm having the kahala."

Jam asked, "What is kahala, anyway? I've been wondering about that since Mr. Wheeler mentioned it."

Dash answered, "A high-quality amberjack that prefers

traveling in dense schools, making it an excellent breed for domestication and farming. It is used primarily for—"

Ping interrupted ecstatically, "Sashimi!"

"As Ping said." After a pause, Dash told them briefly about her morning, ending with, "And on the way down here, Byron was telling me about the minimum wage in America." She turned to Byron. "I have always been puzzled by the American argument over the minimum wage. If it is such a good idea, why is it not several hundred dollars an hour?"

Byron eyed her like she was crazy. "Obviously businesses couldn't afford to pay that much."

Dash pursued the matter with the same focused energy she brought to all her interests. "So, is there a discrete indivisible step function at thirty dollars and one cent?"

Byron's face registered blank puzzlement. "A discrete what?"

Ping pointed her fork at him. "A discrete indivisible step function! Don't you know what that is?"

Jam touched Byron gently on the arm. "Do not let her give you a hard time. She doesn't know what a discrete indivisible step function is either." Jam dipped a thick piece of lobster in butter as she continued, "I don't know either, of course. Dash just says things like that from time to time."

Dash leaned forward. "Hey, not fair." She turned to Byron. "So, in California, is there an indivisible break between thirty dollars and thirty dollars and one cent, such that at thirty dollars all businesses are able to pay the minimum wage, but at thirty dollars and one cent all businesses are not?"

Byron shrugged curtly. "Well, no."

"So, business failures and job losses are a continuous function as the minimum wage goes higher? Would there be more businesses and more employment if the minimum wage were lower? Are there many unemployed people in California and Portland at this time?" At Byron's look of disgust, she explained, "I am just trying to understand the mathematical underpinnings of your belief system."

Byron glared. "I see you're one of those libertarian types."

Dash saw another tall shadow, undoubtedly another American, materialize behind her to the left. She heard Colin speak.

"I doubt Dash even knows what a libertarian is."

Byron looked up at the newcomer, and somehow his pasty skin grew paler. "Mr. Wheeler?" He rose rapidly from his seat.

Colin raised an eyebrow. "And you are?" he asked as he offered his hand.

"Byron Schultz, sir. I'm Dr. Dash's intern."

"Ah. Blue state?"

"Yes, sir. California."

"Well, you won't find any libertarians here."

Byron scowled as he sat back down. "The whole Brain-Trust is a hotbed of libertarians."

Colin gestured at the three women at the table. "Not here. You won't find three people less interested in politics anywhere, Byron. Mind if I join you?" He pulled over a chair from the nearest table without waiting for an answer. "Of course, you're partly right. There are a lot of libertarians on the BrainTrust. Quite ironic, actually, considering that the BrainTrust's basic political structure is that of a corporate dictatorship."

Ping laughed. Byron looked alarmed. Jam and Dash, who had lived under dictatorships, looked horrified. Colin looked at the range of expressions and joined Ping in laughter. "Corporate dictatorship. Here's the bottom line: if there's someone on board we don't like, we send them back where they came from."

Byron leaned forward. "I've heard that on your ferries, if they find a stowaway, they just toss 'em overboard into the ocean."

Jam quietly hunched over and looked down at her plate. "Not true," she whispered.

Colin watched her as he answered, "I've heard that too. Both Huffington and Drudge agree that we secretly slaughter hundreds of refugees. Surely they could not possibly both be wrong, could they?" Colin's expression turned sour. "Nonsense, Byron. Our official policy is to return stowaways to the port they originated from once they get here. In practice, it's sufficiently hard to sneak onto our ferries that the successful few almost always find jobs on board. Employers often line up at the dock to talk to stowaways about job opportunities. Because..." he paused and looked around the table to make sure everyone was paying attention as he revealed a secret truth, "a successful stowaway has a characteristic even more important than genius." He sat back in his chair, waiting to be prompted.

Jam quivered, all her muscles taut, but Dash broke first. "Tell us," she demanded.

"Grit," he said simply. "The relentless pursuit of one's

goal even if one has to cross continents and oceans to achieve it. People with grit can achieve the impossible." He looked at Jam. "Isn't that right, Ms. Yousafzai?"

Grit... Jam ran her finger across her scarred cheek. The memories came at her, and the world and her friends faded from her sight. She flashed back.

Evening turning to night. Jamal, her husband, gone again. The sound of angry voices. Jamal crashing through the door. Rage in his eyes. A fist swinging at her.

Dodge, dodge, block. His anger growing with each missed swing. Dodge. *Don't trip!* The giant ring on his finger, on his fist, in her face. No!

She was dazed, but she was angry too, so she fought. And when it was over and he was curled sideways on the floor screaming, she took the emergency savings stashed behind the flour crock and dragged herself numbly out of her village into the abysmal darkness.

Ping waved a hand just in front of her nose. "Hey, girl, where'd you go?"

Jam's hand flashed as she knocked Ping's away. She touched her scar again.

Ping asked, "Where'd you get that, anyway?"

"My husband," Jam mumbled.

"You hit him back, right?"

Jam raised her hand, examining it closely as she closed

it in a fist. "I was a Pakistani commando! What did he expect me to do?" She looked at Colin. *Grit.*

She knew where she needed to go, but she did not have enough money to get there. She did not have a passport or a letter of recommendation. All she had was her training, but it would be enough.

She remembered leaping off the dock next to the ferry that carried excited new employees to the BrainTrust, and as the ship left the port, she remembered climbing ever so quietly up her rope on the starboard side, and rolling over the gunwale, soaked and shivering, to fall onto the deck. She no longer had any money, but she still had a few dried dates and a soggy biscuit in her pack. Perhaps she could sneak into the bathrooms for water? It would be enough.

She thought of the bosun finding her as she dozed under the tarp covering a deck winch spare. He ordered her out onto the deck, and she explained that she had been a Pakistani commando and she could do security work, and he eyed her skeptically. He gave her a meal and escorted her back onto the deck to demonstrate her hand-to-hand skills with the security chief while the captain watched. After she threw the chief five times and gave him a black eye (for which she apologized), the chief and the captain and the bosun called the BrainTrust. "Boss," the captain said, "we have another sob story for you. Yeah, real grit, if it's true."

Grit. Yes, that was the word he had used.

The chief muttered, "I don't get it. She's graceful and all.

I mean, it's like fighting a ballet dancer, but she's not very fast, so you can see her move—flow, really—from block to attack and back again. She's so slow, she should be easy to take no matter how graceful. But somehow she always has an arm or a leg in position to mess you up, or she's not there anymore. How does she do that?"

The captain chortled. "You don't know? It's easy. Bruno, she starts throwing the block before you start throwing the punch. You have a tell."

"I do not have a tell!" Bruno objected. "Nobody's spotted a tell since high school! I do not have a tell!"

"That's fine," the captain said. He jerked his thumb in her direction. "Tell her that." He turned back to the phone and listened briefly. "No, she surrendered peaceably when we found her. I suspect she could have taken us all, locked us in a hold, and commandeered the ship. Is that laughter? You sound like you're choking. Yeah, it's funny if you're a thousand miles away, I suppose. What? Put her in with Ping? Ping's already got a roommate. A bot wrangler. What are you complaining to me for? Ok, I'll shuffle 'em. In with Ping she goes. Yeah, yeah, right next to that Dyah Amabara-something girl. The doctor. She seems pleasant. Very polite. As you wish."

Jam squeezed her eyes together, and once more shook herself back into the present. She caught Colin's eyes with her own. She silently mouthed the words: *It was you. It was you.*

Colin smiled mischievously. Jam rubbed her scar.

Dash interrupted the unspoken conversation. "Jam, I have offered before, and I offer again. Would you please let me fix your cheek? It would be quite easy."

Jam pulled her hand away from her face. "It helps me remember." She put her hand down and leaned toward Dash. "Why don't you get your eyes fixed so you don't have to wear those ridiculous glasses anymore?"

Dash turned away. "I, uh…"

Ping interjected smugly. "I know why. I bet she thinks they make her look older."

Jam looked at Ping, then back at Dash. "Is that true?"

Dash bowed her head. "Without them, I look too young to be a doctor. Even in Bali, I still looked like a college student. And to American eyes, I look—"

"Like jailbait," Ping interjected brightly. "Same as I do." Her smile turned wolfish. "Of course, in my line of work it's helpful to look harmless. Then, *Ka-Pow*! But it's probably different for Dash."

Dash squared her shoulders. "The glasses and the lab coat grant me the appearance of maturity I deserve."

Ping interpreted this for everyone. "She wears the glasses so her patients don't argue with her so much."

Dash nodded her head sheepishly. "That too."

A moment's silence filled the air, then Ping picked up the thread of conversation that had been dropped. The thread Jam had so neatly dodged. "Jam, we were discussing your husband. The one who hit you, you know." She pointed at the scar. "What did you do to him when he did that to you, Ms. Pakistani Commando?"

Jam looked down at her hands, now clasped hard together. She mumbled an answer only Ping could hear.

Ping clapped. "Do you have a picture of him? In case he ever shows up here, I mean. I want to spot him right off." Ping reached out very slowly and lightly touched Jam's scar. "I think he deserves one of these, too. Dash, as a surgeon, could you teach me how to cut a cheek just that way?"

Dash frowned at Ping. "I still have not heard what she did to him. Jam?"

"Tell her," Ping demanded. "Don't mumble."

Jam looked at Ping. "He won't show up here." She delicately took a sip of tea and looked at Dash. "I broke his nose." She took another sip and looked at Ping. "He wouldn't dare come after me here."

Jamal passed through the metal detectors aboard the *Elysian Fields* and hurried toward his luggage. A security woman stared at the x-ray screen as his bags passed through the machine, then at him, then back at the screen. He was suddenly glad he was wearing Western clothes, from the obscenely colorful Hawaiian shirt to the stupid flip flops his heels kept stepping sideways out of. Ridiculous! He raged within, but he smiled placidly, like a harmless tourist. Idiots! Of course, they were all heathens, so what could he expect?

The woman in the security uniform frowned at him. "There's a knife in there, right? You'll have to pull it out and show me."

He pushed the earplug from his phone deeper into his ear and asked the phone to retranslate her question. "A work of art," he explained. As the phone translated for her, he continued, "Hundreds of years old." He hoped the translation sounded proud, because he was. His *chura* was indeed a work of art, handed down from his father and his father's father. He opened the bag and removed the weapon reverently. "Should I withdraw it from its sheath?"

The woman sighed. "It's just short enough to pass our standards, so I'm not going to confiscate it. You understand?"

Jamal nodded vigorously, almost bowing. "Thank you. You are a kind person." Idiots! Still, it was fortunate he owned a *chura* rather than a longer *peshkabz*. It would have been annoying if his knife had been confiscated. He would have had to kill his wife with a Western kitchen knife. It just would not have been proper.

Jamal grabbed his bag and hurried to catch up with his younger brother Amu, who was standing next to his best friend Marjan. He was delighted to have Marjan along on this journey of honor. Not only was he as big as a water buffalo, but Marjan also happened to be Jameela's brother.

Upon reaching his companions, he dropped his bag on a chair and unzipped it. He held the *chura* in his hands, reluctant to put it back in the bag. The elephant-tusk hilt was old and worn, but Jamal had polished it religiously every night since that night. The night she'd broken his nose. And although the *chura* was designed as a stabbing weapon—the curved blade tapered to a reinforced tip, originally designed for penetrating a knight's steel armor— he had also sharpened the blade's razor edge. Though the blade remained sheathed, in his mind he could see that edge, and taste the blade's hunger for his wife's blood. He grabbed the hilt to pull it forth.

Marjan hissed, "Are you crazy? Don't pull that out here!" He looked around fearfully. "There are video cameras everywhere!"

Jamal squeezed the hilt, furious and determined to do as he would, no matter what Marjan said. But a dollop of sanity returned. He caressed the handle for a moment, then tucked the sheathed knife into his waistband and pulled his Hawaiian shirt over it.

Amu pointed to a passageway off to the right. "I think our rooms are that way." As he turned down the passage, he pointed again. "There's an available hooker!"

A woman with long strawberry-blond hair wearing a cherry-red bikini top and a black microskirt tottered down the hall on red wedgies. Seeing a man come out of a room, she waved. "John!"

John, seeing her, smiled and held his arms wide. The woman demonstrated extraordinary grace and balance as she ran on her high heels. They wrapped each other in a tight embrace.

Amu was irritated. "This ship is full of hookers, but they all have customers all the time."

Jamal growled. "Forget the hookers, Amu. We're here on holy business."

"But this is the only chance I'll ever get to have a Western hooker!" He tapped the pocket where he kept the twenty-dollar bill his uncle had given him. "Well, two hookers. I have enough money for two."

"Stay focused! You can look for hookers after we find Jameela."

"I guess," Amu grumbled.

A teenage brunette in a purple G-string and sneakers passed them going the other way. Amu watched forlornly.

Now Marjan complained at him. "Keep your eyes on the directions." He looked up and down the hall. Vidcams were angled at both ends of the passage.

The ever-present vidcams launched Marjan into an old complaint. "I still don't understand how you expect to trap my sister, kill her, and get away without getting caught."

Jamal smiled for the cameras. "And I keep telling you, I hope to get caught. I am eager to be recognized as I fulfill my mission of honor." He paused. "You've read the descriptions of the BrainTrust as thoroughly as I have. They don't have jails or real courts or any way of punishing people except by making them pay money." They turned down another corridor and into an enormous elevator. Amu punched the button for their deck. "After they catch us, what will they do? Their own writings tell us they will send us back to Pakistan for judgment."

"Where they'll put us in jail for forever when the Brain-Trust demands justice."

"Where they'll send us back to our own village. We'll be celebrated as heroes," Jamal countered. He tapped Marjan on the shoulder. "I understand your fear, my friend, but it is baseless. The BrainTrust is not some mighty nation, able to bend our government to its will. It is just a bunch of big boats full of infidels, infidels so deep in sin that even infidel countries view them as heretics. The BrainTrust may request that a Pakistani judge treat us as he would a heathen, but our country will insist on showing the world it is an independent sovereign state. Once we get to

Pakistan, we'll be home in a week." Home, and basking in their victory against Marjan's humiliating sister.

Dash paced back and forth at the front of the empty conference room, pushing her hair back time and again. The introductory slide of her presentation showed steady on the screen, except that from time to time she clicked rapidly through the slides to find and scrutinize a particular image and silently mouth the words that went with it. She was scheduled to defend her detailed proposal for human trials in a few moments. Three senior members of the medical research department would tell her what she had overlooked and leave her with a lengthy list of tasks still to be done before she could even dream of starting.

She was deep in review of the patient selection process when she heard someone tap on the frame of the open door. She half-jumped out of her skin.

Amanda.

"Here early, are we?" Amanda made a droll face. "Well, I was much the same the first time I went through one of these trials-by-fire." She dropped into a chair and thumped a thick sheaf of paper onto the table. "Your proposal." She tapped the paper. "I find I still prefer reviewing these proposals on paper, even after all these years. Someday the admins are going to sneak into my office, hijack my printer to the dumpster, and leave me helpless." Her eyes were alight with laughter. Dash wished she understood the joke.

Dr. Austin Williams joined them moments later. His skin was much darker than Dash's own, he was heavyset, and he had short curly black hair and a jovial expression. Dash suffered a moment's panic. Her first meeting with him had taught her to fear his gentle eyes. After the niceties of polite conversation had been fulfilled, he moved swiftly to questions that were sharp and insightful. Which was fine, but those questions all too frequently focused on the aspects of her plan for which she had fewest answers. She found herself having to thank him for embarrassing her—a most uncomfortable situation. He smiled kindly at her as he slid into a seat, but she was not fooled.

The last member of the committee popped into the room at exactly the appointed moment for the meeting to begin. He moved with hurried grace, as if he had some-where else he needed to be if only people would let him get on with it. Dash had come to realize that this was a correct interpretation of his situation most of the time.

Dr. Galen Blanchard was only a couple years older than Dash herself, she suspected. His thick black eyebrows were perhaps his most striking feature, set in a pale European face. Dash rather thought that Byron might grow to be like him in a few years. They not only had many physical simi-larities, they shared the same level of intensity and focus. Galen spoke in such quick clipped phrases that she had trouble following him. Amanda had explained that he had been born in France but grew up in New York City, and therefore could not help himself. Dash's earlier meeting with him had been very brief. He had transferred a page of notes to her tablet, apologized, and gone off to address the next item on his agenda. The notes had been useful, though she had thought they might have been more useful still with a little explanatory conversation.

Dash knelt next to the corner of the table and picked up a pink box. "Welcome, and thank you for coming." She placed the box on the table and opened it for their inspection. "I brought donuts, if anyone would like one."

Before the others could move, Dr. Blanchard plucked a glazed pastry from the box. "Thank you," he mumbled as he took the first bite. "No breakfast."

Dr. Williams took a lazy moment to consider the array before selecting a solid chocolate donut. "I don't know that we'll be here long enough to finish these," he said in a way that Dash found ominous, "but thank you for the thought."

"Of course," Dash answered stiffly.

After Amanda demurred, Dash began her presentation. "First let me talk about the design of the telomere replicators. The CRISPIER, as you know—"

Dr. Williams coughed. "Excuse me, Dr. Dash, we are all very interested in hearing your presentation, but why don't we pass Amanda's delightfully archaic paper copy of your proposal around and sign off before we get into the details?" He smiled broadly. "Amanda's been following your development of the plan quite closely, has she not?"

Dash stared at him. "Yes…"

"And I have read it thoroughly. On my tablet, of course," he said, looking at Amanda with humor. "Blackie, I'm sure you've read it in penetrating detail as well, haven't you?"

"Of course," Dr. Blanchard said abruptly. "I have notes—"

"Yes, certainly," Williams interrupted. "But did you find the plan fundamentally sound?"

"Well, yes." Blanchard looked flustered.

Williams pulled himself to the table. "Well, then." He

pulled an old-fashioned ink pen, black with a hint of gold inlay, from his pocket with a flourish. "Let us get on with it." He handed the pen to Amanda, who signed the top page of the document. Williams pulled the document over to himself and signed, again with a flourish. "Blackie?" he asked, shoving the pen and paper his way.

Blanchard stared at him for a second, then smiled. "Of course."

Williams took the pen and the paper and laid them in front of Dash. "These are yours." He straightened. "Now, I'm sure your presentation would be even more enjoyable over drinks, perhaps in Ten-Forward on *Gplex I*. That would be a more suitable venue than this barren conference room. Any objections?"

Blanchard jumped out of his seat. "That sounds very nice, Dr. Williams, but I really have to—"

"Of course," Williams interrupted soothingly. "You have to go." He waved to the door. "See you for Akston's progress report this afternoon."

Blanchard said on his way out the door, "Dr. Ambarawati, I'll send you my notes for your consideration." And he was gone.

Williams turned. "Amanda?"

"I think a drink would go quite well with the rest of our discussion."

"Dash?"

Dash was still trying to grasp what had happened. She had the required three signatures on her proposal, so she guessed it was approved. "I... Yes, that would be nice."

Amanda rose from the table. In the tone of a teacher enlightening a student she observed, "Dash, please note:

the review and approval of a research proposal of this nature has to be serious, but it does not need to be formal." She looked into the distance at phantom people she had argued with in the past. "At least not here."

Dash gave her a partial bow. "Yes. Thank you, *Bu* Amanda."

It turned out that her presentation was, indeed, better discussed over drinks. Even if her own drink was just a Coke with a cherry on top.

4

A LITTLE TROUBLE

It ought to be remembered that there is nothing more difficult to take in hand, more perilous to conduct, or more uncertain in its success, than to take the lead in the introduction of a new order of things. Because the innovator has for enemies all those who have done well under the old conditions, and lukewarm defenders in those who may do well under the new. This coolness arises partly from fear of the opponents, who have the laws on their side, and partly from the incredulity of men, who do not readily believe in new things until they have had a long experience of them.

—Machiavelli, *The Prince*

When she arrived in the cafeteria with Byron by her side the next day, Dash saw Jam sitting alone at their normal table. Dash asked, "Where's Ping?"

Jam shrugged. "She said she's bringing a surprise."

Dash sat down. "Well, I hope she hurries. I have a meeting with a member of the Food and Drug Administration shortly."

Byron looked at her in astonishment. "The FDA is coming to hear about your work?"

Dash shrugged. "When *Bu* Amanda told me about it, she was surprised too. Her comment was, 'Nothing good can come of it.'"

Byron looked excited. "I don't see why not. Maybe they want to fast-track your therapy for certification."

"*Bu* Amanda thought it was more likely they wanted to sabotage me. She pointed out that the FDA did not even acknowledge aging as a condition for which treatment was appropriate until 2031, when a public outcry arose because the media found out that people were actually living longer if they illegally took a well-known decades-old diabetes medication rumored to have longevity properties. *Bu* Amanda recommended that I be polite to the FDA, but get them off the BrainTrust as quickly as possible so I could get back to work."

Byron could not help arguing. "Regulators are not all bad. Sure, they get carried away sometimes, but..." his voice faded as he looked at the approaching Ping.

Ping was pulling a black metallic set of interlocking tubes from a back harness. She shook the metal tubes several times; they popped out of their original positions and locked into new ones. Soon the assembly was taller than she was. She hoisted one end onto her shoulder. After swaying under the burden for a moment, she adjusted her balance and pointed it toward the windows.

"See my Big Gun?" she asked excitedly.

Jam pursed her lips. "I see a BT12 PGM Autolauncher with both IR and radar targeting."

"That's what I said! It's my Big Gun."

Byron shrank down in his seat as if trying to use the table to shield himself. "Could you please put that away before someone gets hurt?"

"Don't worry, I left the missiles in the armory. It can't hurt anybody."

Dash countered. "If you swung it the wrong way, you could bash someone in the head. I second Byron's request. Please put it away." As Ping's face turned sorrowful, Dash softened her tone. "It is a very pretty Big Gun. I have no doubt it would be quite effective for, uh…"

Jam finished the compliment. "Blowing up small boats and slow aircraft."

Ping pushed a hidden locking button with her thumb and shook the weapon back down to backpack size. "We're ready now."

Byron was slowly turning purple. "Ready for what!? You got that out of an onboard armory? What are you doing with an armory on the ship? If you shoot a gun in these steel passageways, the bullets'll ricochet off the walls and kill a dozen people!"

Jam interceded. "Which is why the guns are locked in an armory. In a Condition Red Defense of Ship, the armory is unlocked. The crew, including Ping and myself, can retrieve our assigned firearms. And any residents who brought their own guns aboard can fetch them as well, for the duration of the emergency."

Byron pushed. "So people can just wander the passages with guns?"

This time Ping replied. "Only during Condition Red. And of course, the tourists on *Elysian Fields* are not allowed to bring guns on board at all. Only the crew and residents are allowed to participate in the defense of the ship. Letting tourists have guns would just be crazy."

This left Byron speechless for a moment, but it did not last. "Defense of Ship? Defense from whom?"

Dash gave him an answer she thought he might appreciate. "Defense from the Red Party that runs your federal government, for one. If you remember your history, the President-for-Life was planning at one point to put soldiers aboard and forcibly evict everyone from the BrainTrust."

Ping hissed, "Piracy, plain and simple."

Byron shook his head. "That was a long time ago."

Dash's phone rang. She glanced at the text message she'd just received. "I have to go." She looked remorsefully at the other tables where people sat eating and chatting. "I guess I'll eat later. I need to meet our guest from the FDA."

Jam pushed away from the table. "It would be good to stretch my legs. May I come with you?"

Dash motioned for her to come along. The two of them departed, leaving Ping smiling brightly at Byron, who glared back and demanded the last word in the argument. "Physical assaults like that just don't happen in modern times."

Dash and Jam walked outside onto *Chiron's* sun-washed boat dock, and Dash pointed to a yacht docked at one of the slips. It seemed tiny, though Dash supposed that just about any yacht would look small tied up alongside a BrainTrust isle ship. "That must be his boat."

As they approached the dock, Jam looked at the yacht in puzzlement. "Why did he come in a boat? Why not a copter?"

A head sporting sandy short-cropped hair appeared on the ladder from belowdecks. As he climbed into full view, he said, "What a great excuse to take my yacht out for a spin!" He reached the stern and jumped lightly across to the dock. "I'm Dr. Jack Keller from the Food and Drug Administration. And you must be—"

"Call me Dash," she said as she shook his hand heartily. "And this is Jam."

Jam saw a frown cross his face for a moment before the smile came back. Addressing Jam, he asked. "Are you coming with us to talk about telomeres as well?" As Jam laughed at this, another man came down the ladder from the yacht's wheelhouse. Something about him struck Jam as odd. The only thing she consciously saw that seemed out of place was that he was wearing combat boots instead of deck shoes. Jam spoke a little distractedly. "No telomeres for me today, exciting as that sounds." She was about to explain that she had to go start her peacekeeping shift when the man in the boots started to loop a loose line around a cleat—a simple loop, not a cleat hitch as she'd learned was proper on her trip across the Pacific. "I have some errands to do."

The man with the line glared at her, clearly wishing she'd go away. "Who're you?" he demanded.

"Friend of Dr. Dash. You?"

Jack interrupted. "He's my crew. Kurt." After a moment's pause, he turned. "Anything wrong, Kurt?" Kurt replied gruffly, "Everything's fine, Mr. Keller."

Jam's eyes narrowed. *Mr.* Keller? A strange lack of courtesy...unless Jack Keller was not really a doctor.

At that moment Kurt turned toward the ladder to go belowdecks. As the breeze ruffled his jacket, Jam saw a bulge outlined at the small of his back. A whiskey flask? A bottle of Love Potion Number 9? Or a pistol?

Something was not right here.

Jack frowned at her; apparently he wished she were gone as well. When Jam showed no inclination to depart, he turned to Dash. "I was going to ask you to come aboard for a cup of real mainland coffee, but we should probably be on our way." He bowed to Dash and waved his hand toward the nearest passage. "Lead on."

On impulse Jam said, rather too loudly, "You know, this is a delightfully sunny spot. I believe I shall sit and read a bit." She strolled to where she could lean her back against a bulkhead, slid down to the deck, pulled her tablet from a pocket, and began to peruse a romance novel.

A couple minutes later Kurt came partway up the ladder and saw her. After a long considering moment he smiled, sort of. "Well, if you're a friend of Dr. Dash and you're gonna hang out here a while, you might as well come aboard. There are more comfortable places you can sit, and I'm making coffee."

Jam smiled innocently back. "That would be great." She hated coffee, but she doubted they'd get that far. She rose languidly from the deck and kicked off her shoes. The soles of her sneakers were too soft if she needed to kick, so she hated wearing them in a fight.

Kurt offered a hand to climb aboard and she accepted.

"The galley is beyond the salon." He gestured down the ladder. "Ladies first." She went down into the salon, wholly outfitted in lustrous redwood, and took several steps toward the doorway at the far end. As Kurt came down the stairway she raised her right arm; her glittering bracelet of shiny silver disks let her look behind her. "Is the galley that way?" she asked, pointing forward.

He reached the bottom of the ladder and turned. "Huh?" he asked.

She continued to keep her back to him as she walked partway into the galley. "This way?"

"Uh, yeah," he replied in another brilliant conversational foray.

She watched in the disks as he pulled a delightfully wicked-looking Ka-Bar from beneath his jacket. Very embarrassing. She hadn't spotted the knife; she'd expected him to go for the gun. Well, on the bright side, this would save her a search of the galley, since she was going to need a knife in a few moments anyway.

Kurt leaned forward, bringing the knife up. Jam leaned forward too and kicked back with her heel, very glad indeed she'd ditched the sneakers.

Kurt gave a satisfying grunt as her foot drove into his solar plexus. She spun to chop his throat. This encouraged Kurt to follow up with a guttural cough. There was a sharp snap as she took his knife-hand in hers and broke his wrist against a convenient counter, bringing him to new heights with his virtuoso performance of a scream of pain. The knife clattered to the floor. She removed the gun from the small of his back—a nice Daewoo 9mm, a professional's piece for all that Kurt had not shown much skill. Perhaps he, like her husband, assumed she was easy because she was a woman. "*Hmpf*," she grunted. She snatched up the knife and poked him deeper into the galley. "I used to be a Pakistani commando," she growled angrily. "Why don't people take me seriously?" She reined in her anger and switched to a chattier voice. "They teach us many interesting interrogation techniques in the commandos. I'm sure you'll enjoy learning them. They should be useful in your line of work."

After sitting him down on the closest chair she swapped the knife for the gun, making sure he could see the barrel pointed at his chest. That would encourage him not to offer her a distraction as she rifled the drawers in search of zip ties. She conveniently found them in the second drawer she opened—big thick ones, no doubt originally intended for Dash.

After zip-tying him to the chair, she swapped the gun for the knife once more and picked up where she'd left off. "You know, since we're not actually aboard the BrainTrust, we are free of their rules and conventions on handling prisoners." She leaned over, putting her face into his. She smiled for him, letting a slightly crazed excitement light her eyes. "We are on our own to work out our relationship as we see fit."

Kurt opened his mouth to object, but the serenity of her madness seemed to stop him. She tapped him lightly on the forehead with the flat of the blade, and brought the point to hover over his left eye. "What's that, Kurt? You disagree? What difference do you think your opinion makes?"

Jam knew, of course, that she would be in serious trouble when her bosses found out about this little escapade, especially if they decided she'd gone as crazy as Kurt thought. But after watching Kurt's expression change, she concluded that she'd accomplished her goal. She knew that he believed that *she* believed what she'd said. Good enough—now they could talk.

After Kurt had told her everything he knew—a kidnapping attempt on Dash, he didn't know who was paying or why, very disappointing—Jam made a sandwich. "This is very good roast beef," she remarked conversationally. "You know, on the BrainTrust we don't get roast beef as often as I'd like. It is all about the fish." She took a bite. "Now, the seafood is good, even excellent, but really, you can only eat so much lobster before you get tired of it." Kurt, now gagged in addition to being zip-tied, was just staring at her when they heard footsteps. They heard Jack's voice. "Why don't you come aboard?"

Dash replied shyly, "Ok."

Jack continued, "We have some really nice roast beef." *Well,* Jam thought, *less than he thinks.*

Dash spoke with caution, "I am afraid I don't eat beef, Dr. Kelly."

Jam shook her head. Ooops, a serious *faux pas* there, Dr. Kelly.

He recovered smoothly. "Of course. We also have fined aged Swiss cheese. We can have a snack before we depart. Kurt?" he yelled. When no response greeted him, he muttered. "Hang on a minute. Let me find him. Kurt!" he called again as he passed through the doorway into the galley and saw Jam.

She swiftly pulled him out of view from the salon and struck him in the throat. This caused him to gurgle, much as Kurt had done earlier. After slamming his head against the bulkhead for good measure, she settled him next to Kurt and zip-tied them together. Jam stepped into the salon with Dash.

"Jam!" Dash cried. "What are you doing still here?"

"Just talking with Kurt. He's a great conversationalist."

Dash put her hand over her mouth. Jam was thankful she didn't actually giggle. "Kurt?" Dash repeated in disbelief.

"It surprised me too."

A hoarse cough came from the other room.

Jam ducked halfway into the galley. "Oh my, that's a mess". She blocked Dash's view and pulled out the Ka-Bar. "Dash and I should leave you two to clean this up." She thrust the knife in Jack's direction. "What do you think, Dr. Kelly?"

"Go," he croaked, loudly enough for Dash to hear.

"Great," Jam said lightly. "Perhaps we'll see you again later." The knife disappeared once more beneath Jam's jacket as she turned back to Dash. "There's some consider-able cleanup to do in the galley," Jam explained. "They'll be tied up for a while working out the problem." She pulled out her cell and typed quickly. "There. Now they'll get the help they deserve."

As they stepped off the yacht Jam started to hum, a beautiful bright melody, then as quickly stopped.

Dash noted the abruptness. "You should sing more often. Everyone agrees you have a beautiful voice."

"I don't sing," Jam said repressively. Confessing more than she intended, she continued, "Not since my wedding day."

They continued to walk away. After a time, Dash frowned in puzzlement.

Jam asked, "What's wrong?"

"Dr. Kelly seemed surprisingly unfamiliar with my work."

Jam waved it away confidently. "Tongue-tied."

"You think he was attracted to me?" Dash ran her fingers through her hair, pushing it back from her face.

Jam gave her a measuring look. "You are a beautiful woman, in your own excessively cute but very professional way. He is a man. Of course he was attracted to you."

Dash formed an "Oh" with her mouth. "Goodness. Was he trying to…'hit me up?'"

"Yes," Jam agreed. Now her voice took on the satisfied warmth of a purring kitten. "I'm sure that's just what he was doing."

The Chief Advisor rose from his desk in fury. "What?"

"Goons," the calm voice said over the phone. "Two of them. Paid to kidnap Dr. Ambarawati." A pause. "Not up to your usual standards, Mr. Chief Advisor. Shoddy."

"It wasn't me!" the Chief Advisor exclaimed. "Who are they?"

"Well, that's interesting. There was no information on either of them in any of the criminal databases we can access. And they had excellent FDA credentials. They seem to be protected by someone powerful. Perhaps a Chief Advisor?"

"Look, if I were going to kidnap the good doctor, I'd just send a Seal team and be done with it."

"Aha. Of course." Another pause. "So you want these kidnappers brought to justice?"

"Of course I do." The Chief Advisor's voice grew silky. "Why don't you send them to me? I promise to prosecute them to the full extent of the law." And he would, too... after getting as much information on their backers as he could, using interrogation techniques not allowed on the BrainTrust.

"I'll think about it. If we do send them to you, you'll let us know what you find out, won't you?"

"Oh, I can promise you that."

"Good." The voice broke the connection.

The Chief Advisor sat back down. Someone was trying to beat him to the punch. He would have to move up his timetable.

Whichever dictator or tyrant or oligarch was trying to horn in on his action would be dealt with. Harshly.

Colin put down his cell. "So he'll send a Seal team, as we expected. He'll move faster now, though."

Amanda covered her face with her hands, then slapped the top of his desk. "Colin, you have to stop playing games like this!"

He sighed. "Yes, but perhaps not today. This particular game is now running without us. We can let it sweep us away or we can direct it, but we cannot stop it." He stared at the picture adorning his office wall. An isle ship floated on surging water with an enormous, contented-looking, sleepy red dragon draped over it. A tiny girl petted the dragon's tail, which curled down to the sea. Amanda couldn't see it at the moment, but she knew that in the corner of the painting was a dedication, "For my Dragon." It was signed, "Elisabeth". The title of the painting, "Home Defense," glowed on a gold plate beneath. "Since the day we came aboard *GPlex I*, we haven't been able to stop this game."

"Someday you're going to get someone hurt. Someone we care about," Amanda growled.

"Yes," he agreed. "Probably myself, among others."

Her office was austere. Dash suspected that some prison cells had more elaborate decorations. A picture of her parents sat on her desk. A diminutive jade statue of Gane-sha, the Elephant god who served as Remover of Obstacles, god of Wisdom, and Lord of Success rested in the center of a tiny round table. Ping and Jam had announced that she needed more stuff the first time they saw her office, so Ping had supplied her with a pair of swords, a *katana* and a shorter *wakizashi*, on a lustrous lacquered black stand. They were now displayed in solitary splendor on her bookcase, which held no books. The bookcase itself was, in Dash's opinion, an anachronism, but it was well suited to holding a pair of weapons she had no idea how to use.

Jam, more practically, had given her a rich thick rug in tones of red. She'd bought it with her first paycheck from a programmer who was leaving the BrainTrust because his company had IPO'd and he'd made it big. It covered most of the floor beyond Dash's desk. Sometimes when she was alone, she would slip off her shoes and just walk on the plush pile, curling her toes. Heavenly.

But not today. Today she had the task of interviewing the final patient candidates. Apparently she also had the task of soothing Byron, who stormed into her office in a rage. "What is wrong, Byron? Have all our candidates withdrawn?"

Byron growled. "I just hate them all." He clenched both fists. "Have you seen the security guards who've cordoned off our entire research area? To protect our valued guests, they say. I have to show my badge just to get past them."

Dash looked questioningly at him. "You hate our patients?"

"All the billionaires. Nobody deserves to have a billion dollars."

In her head, Dash rifled through the profiles of the candidates. "Carl Kraemer is not a billionaire."

"No," he agreed reluctantly. His expression turned to admiration. "Now, *he's* a real genius. Wow! It's a shame they don't give a Nobel Prize for Mathematics, or he'd have been the winner several times. All our patients should be as worthy as he is."

"If that was the only way to be worthy, we could not afford worthy patients. The funding for his procedure is being supplied by the BrainTrust Consortium itself." She paused, and continued in a mystified tone, "I do not understand why, actually. He's developing a set of equations that describe a radically different way to shape magnetic fields. Interesting enough, I suppose, but what is the purpose?"

Byron took a half step back, affronted. "To further human knowledge, of course. Why would he need any purpose other than that?"

"I guess," Dash replied doubtfully.

"Meanwhile, the rest of them are money-grubbers who steal from the people."

Once more Dash sorted through the candidates in her head. "As nearly as I can tell, several of the others made their money by starting new businesses—or even whole new industries—and creating thousands of jobs. In what way is that stealing?"

"Billionaires!" Byron snorted in disgust. "There just shouldn't be any!"

"So only governments should have billions of dollars?"

"Of course," said Byron. "Only governments look out for all the people's welfare."

Dash was too startled to speak for a moment. She reflected on the endless miseries and thousands of needless deaths the governments of the countries around Bali had inflicted on their people in previous decades. "Your experience of governments is considerably different than mine," she answered cautiously. Before he could reply, she continued, "Has the first candidate arrived? Ben Wilson?"

Byron nodded. "Yeah, Ventures has arrived. So have Pipelines and VBC—Voter Behavior Correction."

"Pipelines?"

Byron blushed. "I keep track of them based on what industry they own."

"Ah." Dash was pretty sure none of her prospective patients actually owned the industries they competed in, but it was a very Byron thing to say. "So, Mr. Wilson is Ventures?"

"Yeah." Byron lowered his voice to a whisper. "You need to be really nice to him."

Again Dash looked baffled.

"He's one of your investors."

"Goodness." Dash pursed her lips in consternation. "Well, send him in, please."

Ben Wilson had lost virtually all his muscle mass to aging. His arms were shriveled folds of skin, where once he'dhad substance. Overall he was skinny as a rail, except for a paunch. As he seated himself ever so carefully, Dash found herself worrying if he would be able to stand up again. He ran his hand across the remaining strands of his wispy hair.

Dash came straight to the point. "I am told that you are one of our investors, Mr. Wilson."

A twinkle appeared in his eye. "Ah, you found me out. I am indeed."

"Did you invest just so you could be a candidate?"

He shook his head. "Certainly not. I'm delighted to be a candidate, but I didn't really expect it." He leaned forward in his chair and said conspiratorially, "Shucks, if it's going to be as dangerous as your huge list of warnings and caveats says, you should probably hold off putting me in the program until you have a replacement angel lined up." He shrugged. "Of course, as you can see from my condition I could pass away at any time, which would also leave you strapped for cash. Tough call you have there, from a financial perspective."

Dash maintained her most professional blank face, though a smile tugged at her lips. "I am not worried about the funding, though I suppose I should be. As it happens, you are a perfect candidate from a physical perspective. You suffer from all the classical symptoms of aging without any special diseases or problems." She looked back at her notes.

Ben said, "In case this makes a difference, I am also handily available as an outpatient. Probably alone among your candidates, I live on the BrainTrust."

Dash looked at him. "Yes, I see here you live on the ship with all the startup companies, the *Dreams Come True*." She shook her head. "I have read that most BrainTrusters who make many millions move dirtside. I understand no amount of money can get you a cabin larger than the standard one."

He nodded. "My cabin is the same size as yours. Much of the value of the BrainTrust comes from the very high density of very smart residents bouncing ideas and opportunities off each other. It's an interesting economic problem, actually. The BrainTrust cannot extract maximum profits without damaging the very characteristic that makes it worth so much." He shrugged. "Of course, being a composable mobile archipelago, there is a solution, and the problem is being solved as we speak. A new purely residential isle ship, the *Haven*, is being built in San Diego by a consortium of billionaires. When it's ready, they plan to attach it to the BrainTrust. You'll be able to buy outright a living space any size you can afford. The investors get first pick, of course. I thought about joining them myself." He smiled wickedly. "Well, I more than thought about it. I bought a stake in the project, including a snug little four-thousand-square-foot apartment." He shook his head. "But that's strictly a rental. I already have guests lined up. Meanwhile, I'm going to stay in my little cabin on *Dreams*. That's where most of my investments are, and the youngsters keep me invigorated. I'm surrounded by other angry young men just like myself."

Angry young men like himself? Dash again controlled her demeanor as she choked back a laugh. "Would you not consider yourself at least an angry middle-aged man at this point in your life?"

Ben laughed so long and hard tears formed in his eyes. "Heavens no, Dr. Dash. Angry *old* men are bitter. Angry *young* men are infuriated by how poorly the world works, how many problems remain to be solved, and they are hot on the path to solving those problems. That's a better characterization of me than the other." He paused reflectively. "Indeed, the number of proper angry young men is small, even among chronologically youthful people. I still have to work to find them, even in the hothouse of creative energy you find here."

His attitude was so odd that Dash wondered if there were something wrong with him mentally, something more subtle than dementia. If the procedure developed complications, what effect would it have on his recovery?

He was watching her, and he deduced that something was amiss. "Do you know why I'm investing in your research? As I explained earlier, I didn't expect to become a patient."

"Because you believe that my therapy can develop into a billion-dollar business?"

"Ah, but it *won't* become a billion-dollar business, Dr. Dash." He paused, relishing the explanation. "It'll become a *trillion*-dollar business. I would enjoy being the world's first trillionaire." He shrugged. "Though, because of the way the profits will be divided, you and the other investors would follow very closely behind me."

"I see." She was about to let him go, but one other question struck her. It was not relevant or necessary, but she just wanted to know. "Tell me, Mr. Wilson, before coming to the BrainTrust, most of your investments were in America, correct? What made you decide to come here in the beginning?"

Ben sighed. "I started thinking about leaving when California hiked the tax rate to seventy percent a few years ago. Fortunately there were enough loopholes, exemptions, and exceptions that I could live with it. The last straw was the billion-dollar lawsuit."

"A billion-dollar lawsuit? What could they sue you for a billion-dollars for?"

"Well, my firm, the Wilson-Petra Fund, had been growing faster every year for almost a decade. Then we had our first bad year. Instead of growing handily, the fund shrank a little bit. The fact that we didn't do as well as projected by the analysts was used in a class action suit as *de facto* proof of managerial incompetence and fraud." He shrugged. "They've been doing that to successful businesses for decades. My grandfather was involved in one of these lawsuits back in 1991, when a Silicon Valley CAD company told the analysts their quarterly profits would go down because they were going to invest more in R&D. This was hardly the decision of incompetent management, but it served the lawyers' purpose. The day after the increase in R&D was announced the stock tanked, and the day after that three different law firms rushed to court to request authority to represent the stockholders in a class action."

"So you lost all your money?" Now Dash had to worry about whether he could pay the bill. It would be very hard on the budget to have to swallow the costs of a bankrupt patient at this stage.

Ben waved the question away. "Not all of it. We settled out of court for half a billion. I sold out as quickly as I could—not very fast, since venture capital is not that good a game for quick churning—but fast enough." He laughed. "Two years later, we doubled our profits over the year prior to the lawsuit." He tapped the table, and his face was alive with wicked joy. "The state of California and the federal government both now want to put me in jail for tax evasion."

"Oh, dear." Every time he answered her and told her not to worry, he introduced a new cause for concern. "Is there any risk that they will take you back in the middle of your therapy?"

Ben was again laughing so hard he had to hold his stomach; the man seemed to spend much of his time laughing uproariously. "Don't let the Feds worry you.

Colin promised them that when the *Dreams Come True* completes its current cruise, it'll call on a port with an extradition treaty. He guaranteed that he'd send me back for trial first thing once they dropped anchor."

Colin again. Dash really had to find out who he was some time. Out of curiosity, she'd looked in the BrainTrust crew directory, but hadn't found him. She refocused on Ben. "But the BrainTrust ships never end their cruises, and never enter ports."

Ben nodded. "Exactly."

A bouncy college-age girl with long golden hair appeared in the doorway. "We'll be right with you," she said brightly. "It'll just take a moment to maneuver Gran into your office. Dash watched in bemusement as two other blond women, one perhaps high school-age, one a thirtyish version of the first, maneuvered a wheelchair into Dash's office. Dash dragged her table with Ganesha off to one side and stood, leaning on the front of her desk to watch the procession.

The youngest, a skinny teenager, looked down in embarrassment. "Sorry," she said, "just getting her settled."

The prospective patient was finally revealed.

An old woman sat in the wheelchair staring off to the side at Dash's empty bookcase. Dash leaned forward "Mrs. Rainer? Anne Rainer?"

The old woman turned her head. Dash could see that Anne had once had hair the same color as her grandchildren's. Seeing Dash, Anne smiled. "Aisha?" she said. "I'm so delighted to see you again." She held out her hand. "You've grown so much. I see you've done well."

Dash was frozen by this speech for a moment. The eldest of the blond attendants explained. "Aisha was one of Gran's favorite students from her time in the Peace Corps."

Dash spoke gently. "I am afraid I am not Aisha, Mrs. Rainer. My name is Dash. Dr. Dash."

"Ah," said Anne Rainer. "I get confused sometimes."

Dash replied, "As do we all sometimes." A moment's silence ensued.

The college-age granddaughter ran a finger gently across Anne's forehead, pushing a strand of hair to the side. "Granma was the first one to diagnose herself with dementia, you know."

"That happens once in a while with the brightest ones." Dash sighed. "Let me be perfectly clear with you all about what is going to happen." She started to explain the steps involved, leading up to the point where Dash would introduce pseudoviruses into their grandmother's bloodstream. The three women followed her words with the intensity of hawks watching a ground squirrel and nodded their heads as she continued her explanation.

Finally the eldest interrupted. "The pseudovirus will lengthen the telomere chains on the nuclei in all Granma's cells."

The middle one took over. "The telomeres, consequently, will give the cells permission to replicate—"

And the teenager finished, "Replacing damaged cells with new ones."

Dash concluded that perhaps Anne's intelligence, which

had enabled her to build a post-social media empire, had run true through two generations.

Dash finished with a warning. "Let us be clear," she said sternly. "Even if this *does* work, there is reason to doubt it will cure her dementia. Of all the test patients we have accepted, Mrs. Rainer is the one least likely to benefit from this therapy. Our procedure here is best thought of as an outlying experiment-within-an-experiment that is already high-risk. Does everyone understand that?"

All three women nodded. For a moment it looked like Anne had nodded in understanding as well, but then she began to gently snore.

The time had come for the Emeryville Chapter of the Earth Liberation Crusade to comport themselves with a modicum of discretion. Peter had told his three friends to cool it with the Green movement slogans. He himself had gone to extreme lengths to hide his real goals and methods, purchasing a t-shirt that had nothing to do with his Green agenda. Now his shirt matched the flags waving informally on a couple of the isle ships, a dark blue ocean and a light blue sky in the background of a bright yellow sunrise. The sunrise backlit the silhouette of a sailing ship with the Statue of Liberty instead of a mast rising from the center.

These people on the BrainTrust thought freedom and liberty were the touchstones of civilization. So hopelessly retro. Freedom, liberty, even the nation-states that tried to defend such things were dead-ends. Only a global government with both the absolute power and the ruthless willingness to suppress the desires of all the greedy humans in order to protect the greater good could successfully deal with the ever-growing host of planet-spanning environmental issues.

Peter was sure that once all the people were united these mobile islands would be destroyed as an obvious part of protecting the planet. Alas, the day of unity continued to lie just a little too far in the distance, like a rainbow that you could drive toward or walk toward but never quite reach. He still didn't understand why a global government hadn't arisen after most of the West Antarctic Ice Sheet broke off and raised sea levels. You'd think that once Miami drowned and the state of Florida shrank to the Everglades Territory people would have woken up, but no. Instead, the Red president blamed the Blues, declared martial law, stacked the Supreme Court, and declared himself President-for-Life to thundering applause. Sigh.

Anyway, Peter had donned one of the symbols of the enemy to keep them confused. His friends, however, just couldn't wrap their heads around the idea of being a little circumspect. After all, they were only smuggling enough explosives to hollow out the entire Los Angeles subway system.

Mary was wearing her own idea of a non-controversial slogan, which was "Go Green or Scream". Paul had demonstrated a reasonable amount of sensitivity with "Don't be Mean, Go Green." Justin was almost as clueless as Mary, with "Demand Clean and Green." Justin of all of them should have been the most prudent, since he was carrying the primary bomb ingredient.

The guard at the x-ray machine looked bemused as

Justin put an entire case of Evian water on the conveyor belt. Justin looked at the guard and blushed. "I just don't trust anybody's water but my own."

The guard shook his head. Another guard whispered to him, and he looked at Mary's hostile expression and the t-shirt and turned cold. Mary's suitcase got the closest scrutiny of all.

As they walked away, Justin whispered to Peter, "That was a nice touch, having Mary distract the guards while I came through with the—"

Peter whispered back urgently. "With the *water*. With the *water*."

"Right. The water."

And it was indeed water, though Justin had enhanced it considerably in his basement. Evian would be surprised to know that they now bottled CHP, otherwise known as concentrated hydrogen peroxide.

Paul caught up with them. "When does the conference start?" Their justification for coming to the BrainTrust was to attend a conference on Making the Oceans Bloom: Life and CO2 Sequestration in the Dead Zone. Peter had the feeling that Paul was almost as interested in the conference as he was in blowing the hell out of a nuke plant. And, Peter confessed to himself, it would have been interesting if it weren't built on the backs of the poor, who had lost their jobs to the BrainTrust robots and would one day lose their lives to radioactive contaminants when something went wrong.

"Conference starts in the morning," Justin told him. "We'll have to attend a few sessions while we're scoping out the ships and finding a suitable reactor target."

Peter growled, "I already told you, I got reliable info on the location of the reactor—at least on the *Chiron*. It's in the middle of the Red Planet deck." He had a friend who worked on the *Chiron*. When Peter had asked, he had answered without hesitation.

Justin scowled. "Yeah, I heard you the first time. I'm telling you it doesn't make any sense. I still think the nukes are in the underwater pylons."

"Which is why we're gonna check it out. If the center of the Red Planet deck is sealed off, we'll know." Peter shook his head in disgust. The immorality of the BrainTrust designers and engineers was unspeakable. The reactor was in the middle of a damn hospital, surrounded by people trying to recover from terrible illnesses and injuries. Might as well put the reactor in the middle of a school! Probably was, come to think of it, at least on the *BrainTrust University*. He clenched his fists. Well, for his own purposes, it was a good arrangement. When the nuke blew, it would take out the thousands of innocent bystanders who had come here to be healed. The mass deaths would put a nice exclamation point on the operation.

Peter reminded everyone of the next step. "Ok, people, you all know the next part, right? Off to the bars to drink."

Everybody nodded their heads. Justin smiled wolfishly. "Vodka. Each of you has to bring a bottle back to our rooms tonight. Two bottles would be better."

Paul threw in the obvious warning. "Only one bottle from each bar we visit."

Mary shrugged. "There're plenty of bars. We could bring a dozen bottles each without anyone being any wiser."

Justin shook his head. "I can't distill that much into pure ethanol with the equipment I'll be able to set up. Don't run a risk by getting more than we can use."

They arrived at the two adjacent cabins they had rented on *Elysian Fields*. Peter realized they still had a couple days' work to do, between scoping out the target, making the ethanol, and the final assembly. At least the rooms weren't too expensive.

Jamal was already swearing as they left their cabin. The rooms here were shockingly expensive, even for someone with the backing of the village elders. He had to find his wife before he ran out of money. He could just see himself confiscating Amu's hooker fund for part of another day's fare.

He considered the possibility that Jameela was not on the BrainTrust, that she had gone elsewhere. But he rejected the notion this time just as he had rejected it so many times before in the past days.

He was near despair. There were fourteen isle ships in the archipelago, with over a hundred and twenty thousand people. There didn't seem to be a central directory. How would he find her? Where in this Satan's city was she? "We'll split up," he announced to his companions. "Amu, you go to the *Chiron*. Marjan, try the *Dreams Come True*. I'll take the university ship." He'd thought about sending Amu to the university ship, but the college coeds looked just like the hookers on the *Elysian Fields*. It would be awkward if Amu insulted the wrong powerful heathen's daughter.

Amu was growing bitter about his luck. They'd been here for several days and he still hadn't had the chance to pick up a prostitute, even though he'd been surrounded by them constantly. His brother was a joyless celibate, unable to think about anything except bringing his heretic wife to justice. Soon, Amu was sure, they'd find Jameela, kill her, and depart, all without even one good bedding.

He'd never have this opportunity again.

Here on the *Chiron* there were far fewer hookers than on the *Elysian Fields*, where virtually all the younger women were advertising their assets. Still, there were a few. As he strolled down the promenade looking for Jameela, he lost his concentration several times as various hookers passed. During one of those lulls in his concentration he noticed a young Japanese girl. At least he thought she was Japanese. She was watching him.

Wearing a sheer white silk camisole cut high above her midriff with very short pants and flip flops, she was surprisingly erotic despite her flat chest and skinny arms and legs. He thought it might have something to do with the strangely disturbing tattoos on her arms. As he drifted in her direction, he could make out the one tattoo as being a dragon. Odd for such a delicate girl to wear such a fierce bit of art. Breathing fire, no less. The other tattoo seemed more in keeping with her appearance, a thin, almost fragile bird taking flight. Even that bird, however, seemed to express a fierceness in its face and beak. Very odd.

Whether it was the tattoos or something else, she was

indeed erotic. She was also the first hooker to show an interest in him. Clearly unattached.

If he'd only had enough money for one hooker he probably wouldn't have considered her, but perhaps she had a voluptuous friend. They could share.

She pulled a piece of her short black hair into her mouth for a second and smiled. Amu smiled back. *This was it*, he realized. He tapped out a quick text to his brother explaining that he had just about finished searching the promenade on the *Chiron* and was going to take a break because he'd found an available hooker. He was going to take this opportunity, so they shouldn't bug him.

She watched him approach, giggling.

Amu spoke to her through the translator on his phone. "Are you available? I have money." He waved his uncle's twenty-dollar bill. "Do you have a friend with a larger bosom?"

The girl's eyes grew wide. "Wow, you sure are forward enough." She glanced around. "You don't want to do it here, they'll arrest us." She laughed. "Catch me if you can." She dodged him and ran past a restaurant and a shop filled with fuzzy stuffed animals you could buy for the patients. She then turned right off the promenade. He sprinted after her.

In moments they had left the promenade behind and were closing on a wide pair of ramps that led up and down to other decks. There were no other people around; Amu figured all the lazy Westerners used the elevators exclusively.

The girl stopped at the ramp and rolled her hips against the railing. "Are you ready to do it?" she asked.

"Yes, yes, *now*," he said as he grabbed her.

She smacked one of his hands away, but he still had a grip on her with the other. "What are you doing? Do you think I'm a hooker?"

Now Amu was confused. "Of course."

She slapped his face. "Idiot." She smacked him again. "Pervert."

"Hey!" Amu had rapidly moved beyond confusion into anger. No woman should slap a man like that! He swung his fist at her face, and although she leaned away from the punch, he connected.

The girl jerked her other arm free and stepped back. A wicked smile lit her face despite the bruise forming under her left eye. "Thank you," she said, and proceeded to put all her weight into a jab to his solar plexus.

Amu found himself unable to breathe, much less defend himself. She kicked him in the knee, and he went down on the other knee with a shriek as she chopped his throat, doubling the difficulty he was having catching a breath.

He watched helplessly as she pushed him onto his back. *How quickly things could go wrong*, he thought almost philosophically. He could only gaze at her as she pulled her right arm back, twisting her whole upper body for a full-strength strike. Only then did he notice the enormous ring she wore. He thought it was going to hurt a lot.

She struck just beneath his eye. His head bounced off the rubbery-but-still-hard deck covering, and suddenly the eye now swelling shut hardly hurt at all.

The girl stood up and pulled her cell from her hip pocket. After she called the police, she muttered something his phone translated as "One down, two to go," but that seemed unlikely.

Jamal once again congratulated himself on his foresight in putting tracking software on Amu's phone. After getting Amu's text, he called Marjan and ran to meet him on the *Chiron's* promenade. They came around the corner just in time to see a skinny little teenage hooker knock Amu to the floor.

Jamal's anger at his brother quickly transformed into fury at the infidel slut who had beaten him. He reached under his shirt for his *chura*, too angry to remember the cameras.

But Marjan had not forgotten. "Jamal!" he hissed. "Stop!" Marjan grabbed Jamal's arm as the vengeful brother pulled the knife from its sheath.

Then Marjan saw more bad news approaching. "Look! Police!"

Jamal froze. He felt his heart skip a beat as he watched two men wearing yellow shirts with black shoulder patches, black pants, and thick leather utility belts hustle toward the girl.

He'd seen a number of people wandering the decks with yellow shirts and black pants, but he hadn't realized they were police till now.

And then he realized how to find Jameela.

He was distracted from this satisfying insight as he watched the police roughly drag Amu to his feet and cuff him. Why were they cuffing *him*, not the slut who'd beaten him so horribly? How could a little teenage slut best his brother like that anyway? And why were the police laughing and chatting with the slut when it was obvious that Amu, who could barely stand, was the victim?

Amu started to fall again and a policeman with rage in his eye dragged him upright. Jamal reached once again for his *chura*, but he realized, without Marjan's warning this time, that it would be a mistake. He let his hand fall. He was here to gain vengeance against a wife who had struck her own husband. He had to let the infidels go. Amu would understand.

At least Amu's denigration had not been wasted. Foolish he might have been, but he had, with this incident, put Jamal on Jameela's track.

It was obvious, once you thought it through. What would that bitch do when she got to the BrainTrust? You had to have a job to be allowed to stay here. Would she work as a waitress? They didn't even have waitresses. The bots did all the food service.

No, Jameela would join the police force. It was her only skill.

All Jamal had to do was check with the police stations, which were surely few in number. At one of them he would find her.

5

FOR A LITTLE TROUBLE MORE

People are invariably smarter than their political beliefs.
—Joe Quirk and Patri Friedman, *SeaSteading*

Dash worked her way through the list of final candidates. She had met Randa Saunders, aka Pipelines, Lucas Kahn of automotive subcomponents, Tom Kovern the financial forecaster, and Ryan Morgan, who stiffly explained that he did voter behavior correction. She was puzzled by this last one until he explained in exasperation that it was like psychohistory, "Not that you would know anything about that, either." Dash had simply raised an eyebrow, and replied, "I doubt Harry Seldon would believe the analogy, Mr. Morgan. Psychohistorical analysis requires aggregation of a population so large it would encompass multiple planets." Morgan was so surprised he almost choked, but after that he behaved quite well.

She was exhausted by the time the last candidate entered her office.

Clint Maupin stepped into the room with the aid of a cane. Two other men accompanied him. The younger one, who had a stocky build and had probably been a football player in his younger days, rubbed his hands together and introduced everyone. "Dr. Dash, this is my father, your patient. I'm Cliff Maupin, and this is our lawyer, Aaron Wright." Dash looked at the lawyer curiously. A lawyer? Why bring a lawyer with them? After they were seated, Dash went into the explanation of what would happen once more. If she had to do this again, she thought she might do well to record it and just play it back. The lawyer peppered her with questions about what could go wrong. "What if the replicating factories didn't stop replicating?" They could not replicate, she explained patiently, outside the hydrogen peroxide bath in which they were prepared. "What if the telomeres got attached to the cell wall, not the nucleus body?" Then we would look upon it with amazement, though it would be as unlikely to be harmful as it would be unlikely to happen in the first place. And so on.

In the end, Clint Maupin leaned forward on his cane and rose. "I'm eager to give this a go," he said. "Any objections?"

Cliff answered smoothly, "No, Dad."

"No, sir," the lawyer confirmed.

As Clint reached the door, his son put a hand on his shoulder. "Aaron and I want just a couple last words with the doctor, Dad. We'll catch up with you in a minute." His father grunted and continued out the door.

As Cliff turned back to Dash, Byron came rushing in,

halting upon seeing that Dash still had company. "Excuse me," he said.

"No problem," Cliff said. "Just give us just a moment." He turned to loom menacingly over Dash. "I and my lawyer just wanted to warn you, Doctor, that if this treatment kills my father, we will sue you till your eyes bleed."

Dash frowned. Cliff was invading her personal space, but she stood her ground. "You clearly have not read the contract, Mr. Maupin."

He took another step closer. Byron straightened, ready to intercede.

Cliff spoke again. "I guarantee we can make you suffer."

She looked down at her list of notes. She did not feel particularly intimidated—all Americans were tall, so she had gotten pretty immune to being massively outsized. But neither did she want to have to deal with this person in the quite possible event of a complicated outcome. "Well, as it happens, it won't be a problem," Dash said firmly. "We already have enough volunteers for our first experiment."

Byron gave a little start of surprise, and Aaron interjected. "Our understanding was that he was already accepted." He paused, clearly relishing his next words. "We naturally expect compensation if he is cut from the program so late in the process."

Dash was contemplating how to express her opinion of this absurdity when Cliff turned to the lawyer and shook his head. "No, no, it's all right." He glanced over his shoulder at Dash. A look of delight filled his face for a moment, then his expression darkened. "Let's get out of here," he said angrily.

Byron watched them thoughtfully as they departed.

"That bastard doesn't want his father to be rejuvenated. He wants his father to die."

Dash looked at Byron in slowly growing horror. "Of course. Oh, my."

"Should we let Mr. Maupin into the program just to stiff his son? Their threats to sue you are pretty foolish out here on the BrainTrust."

Dash sighed, then shook her head. "No. Satisfying as that would be, as we explained in our original request for patients, the families need to be supportive."

"What about Carl?" Byron asked. "He has no family at all."

"At least," Dash answered, "Carl is merely alone. He is much luckier, and a much better candidate, than poor Mr. Maupin."

Byron shook his head. "Poor Mr. Maupin," he muttered. "I guess even being a billionaire doesn't solve all your problems."

"Not if you have family," Dash agreed. "And if you have no family, you have a different kind of problem."

"I still hate them all," Byron muttered.

Amu looked around the room where he would be judged. At least, "a judging" was the best interpretation he could make of the somewhat odd translations his phone was giving him regarding the proceedings. He might not have understood the phone as well as he should. Part of his problem was that his head was still a little muzzy. And his one eye was now throbbing. It was swollen shut.

The room was quite bare. There was no jury box, much less the kind of jury he had seen on Western TV. The only people here were the judge, the hooker, a severe older Western woman in business attire, and a pair of peacekeepers glowering at his side. They acted as if he were the dangerous one, when in fact he was obviously the victim.

The judge—was he a judge?—rapped a wooden block on the table in front of him. "I am Mediator Joshua Pickett. The two parties to the dispute are here?"

The hooker, who was now wearing a peacekeeper's uniform, spoke first. "Yes, Sir. Ping, Sir."

Mediator Joshua's eyes lit with surprise. "Ping. I've heard of you." He turned to Amu. "And you are?"

Amu swallowed hard. "Amu Yousafzai. Sir."

"Amu, then. Very well." Joshua looked at the older woman, whose presence was apparently as mysterious to the judge as it was to Amu. "Amanda? What are you doing here?"

"Just a friend of the mediation, Joshua. I happen to know Ping, since she's stationed on the *Chiron*. And of course a peacekeeper having a violent encounter with a tourist on *Elysian Fields* is a serious matter. Colin thought a member of the Board should be present, and he suggested I attend."

"Colin." To Amu, it seemed that the judge put a great deal of weight into that name, whoever he was. "I see."

Mediator Joshua took a deep breath. "Let's see the video."

The screen on the side wall lit up in a location where everyone could see the events. Amu watched with his good eye as his encounter with the hooker was displayed on the screen: he followed Ping around the corner, confronted her, grabbed her, and got beaten into hamburger. He started to sweat. He was perfectly innocent of any wrong-doing. She was just a hooker! But the video looked very bad. His brother had insisted over and over that punishments on board the BrainTrust were minor matters. They never cut off a person's hand or stoned him to death like they did back home. But watching this replay made him realize just how much trouble he would be in if these people were sufficiently incensed about his assault on a peacekeeper. He shuddered to think what the police would do to a person who attacked a policeman back home. He blurted, "I am sorry. I had no idea your hookers could also work as policemen." Surely they would understand his confusion?

Mediator Joshua stared at him for a long moment, then buried his head in his hands. He muttered something that Amus's translator interpreted as, "This is not funny. This is a serious matter."

The mediator put his hands back on the table, his face once again a mask of objectivity.

"As nearly as I can tell, no damage was done to anyone except for, ahem, Mr. Yousafzai. Correct?"

The hooker sported a good bruise herself. Amu expected her to make an issue of it, but she simply stood at attention and answered, "Yes, sir. No harm, sir."

Joshua turned to Amanda. "Has Amu here received medical attention?"

"Yes, he's received first aid. He'll have a nice scar under that eye, but perhaps it'll serve as a reminder to treat women a bit better."

"Not our business, Amanda." He took another deep breath. "Ms. Ping."

Once more she snapped to attention. "Yes, sir!"

Joshua closed his eyes and rubbed his temples. "Amu was a guest on *Elysian Fields*. Surely you were told on arrival to treat tourists with the utmost respect even when they are being, ahem, irritating. I would have expected that a person with your skills—yes, I told you I've heard about you—a person with your skills would have been able to subdue a guest with less permanent damage."

The hooker leaned her head sideways uncertainly. "He is much larger than I am."

The mediator grunted. Disregarding the hooker's response, he continued, "And loath as I am to defend Mr. Yousafzai here, I am almost sympathetic with his interpretation of your behavior and attire as that of a…"

As the mediator struggled, Amu interjected, "Hooker."

Joshua rolled his eyes. "Indeed." He looked hard at Ping. "As a peacekeeper, you must strive to uphold a higher standard of behavior, even off-duty. Perhaps you could see your way clear to wear a little more clothing in the future?"

Ping frowned. "But if I had done that, he probably would have assaulted another guest. I wasn't dressed any differently than many of the women on *Elysian Fields*."

Amu helpfully offered, "That is true. There are many hookers there."

Joshua winced. Disregarding Amu, he answered Ping. "I see your point."

A moment's silence, and the judge pounded his block of wood again. "Very well. Mr. Yousafzai is to be taken to temporary holding and placed on the first ferry departing for a suitable port to return to his home country. Questions?"

Amu suddenly realized he'd been holding his breath, wondering how many lashes he would be given. They were just sending him home. What a wonderful outcome, just as Jamal had said!

On his way to the ship's brig, the guards allowed him to stop in a restroom. He looked at himself in the mirror. The swelling had subsided somewhat and he could see the outlines of the scar the older woman said he'd have. He rather thought it would give him a rugged look. The girls back home might appreciate this proof of his manly toughness, a reminder of his participation in the faraway battle to regain the honor of his family.

As long as the girls didn't hear that he'd gotten it from a teenage hooker. Perhaps that part of the story need not be told.

The meeting with the Maupins had left a bad taste in her mouth, so Dash was pleasantly surprised when Colin tapped lightly on her door. "I promised you a visit to one of the nuclear reactors. Is now a good time?"

"Oh, my, yes." Dash grabbed her tablet and was out the door.

Down the elevator they went to the orlop deck, which was the bottom-most deck of the entire ship. The theme here in the bowels of the vessel was Tundra. Dash felt a chill just looking at the murals of ice floes covering the walls of the passages. She would have gotten quite lost, she suspected, but Colin moved with the sureness of someone who had spent a lot of time here.

He eventually led her into a tiny room with dimmed lights. A dozen computer screens adorned the walls. Dash glanced at the screens. "Two of them," she whispered to avoid distracting the two men looking intently at one of the displays. "I suspected you had two of them aboard each ship. Are they in the pylons?" The pylons were a pair of dixie cup-shaped protrusions that extended downward from the bottom of each isle ship's hull. Roughly six decks in depth, the pylons were constructed of reinforced concrete just like the hull itself. "The first time I saw the plans for a generic isle ship, I thought the pylons would make excellent places to house compact nuclear reactors." She paused. "Of course, I am sure the pylons are also very helpful in maintaining stability during ocean storms." She glanced mischievously at Colin. "So you did not quite lie to the media about the purpose of the pylons."

Colin ducked his head and gave her an equally mischievous smile. "It would be poor engineering to have the pylons serve only one purpose," he agreed, "though I find that most people think that one purpose is, in general, sufficient."

The taller of the two men turned at the sound of their voices. "Colin?" He peered at them. "Good to see you."

"You too." Colin performed a brief introduction. "Rhett, this is Dash, our newest medical research lead and project owner. She is also a, um, nuclear reactor *cognoscente*."

Rhett was dressed in the style of a cowboy. He wore a western-cut blue shirt which closed with studs tucked into tight black jeans. His boots seemed better suited to the sandy towns and hills of Arizona that Dash had seen in numerous cowboy movies. Of course, the decks of isle ships put no serious demands on any form of footwear; more than one admin in her own research area wore high heels. Dash suspected Rhett had earned those boots the hard way, since his face had the deep lines of someone who had spent much time in the sun.

Rhett looked at her quizzically. "A *cognoscente*, eh? What does that mean exactly?"

"It means I have had the occasional thought that perhaps nuclear reactor technology—at least the technology reported in the media—could be improved upon."

"Indeed. Well, we can always use suggestions for improvements," Rhett answered with good humor. You could tell from the amused expression as his gaze darted to Colin and back to Dash that he wasn't sure whether to take her remark seriously or not. He turned to the other man, who still studied the display. "Lorenzo, we have company. Could you give...ah...Dash...a tour of the facility?" He looked sideways at her. "Not that there is much of anyplace to go on the tour, you understand. This room is the closest we get to the reactors themselves. Robots do all the heavy lifting."

"Of course," Dash acknowledged primly. "Though you do have hatches into the pylons, don't you? Are they large enough for people, or just for robots?"

Rhett looked sternly at Colin. "I thought we were still trying to keep the reactors and their locations under wraps."

Colin held up his hands in surrender. "I didn't tell her anything, Rhett. She figured it all out on her own."

"*Hmph.*"

Dash stepped behind Lorenzo to look at a video display of the area around the core. "Clearly it's in the pylon," she said. "See how the outer wall wraps around in a circle?"

"*Hmph,*" Rhett repeated.

She looked more closely, jumped a bit, and clapped in delight. "And they are molten salt reactors, just as I'd hoped! Lithium fluoride?"

Colin turned away to hide his laughter when Rhett gave him another long look. "Yeah, lithium fluoride."

Lorenzo was staring at her in appreciation. "How did you know?"

Dash pointed to the center of the screen. "I presume that is the core, the thing that almost looks like an over-sized pot with a partially open top?"

Lorenzo nodded.

"It is operating at normal atmospheric pressure, no high pressure or boiling water." Dash looked over at Colin and Rhett. "Molten salt is the only sensible choice. You cannot afford a nuclear disaster, and molten salt—if done correctly—is inherently safe. Since the fuel is already liquid, it cannot melt down, and at standard atmospheric pressure there is little risk of an explosion. Particularly since the liquid expands if the liquid core overheats, creating a longer mean free path for the neutrons, reducing reactions, and cooling the liquid. You could have a complete power failure and a full containment breach and it still wouldn't harm anything outside the pylon."

Colin could no longer control himself. He burst into outright laughter. "See? A *cognoscente.*"

Dash continued as if Colin hadn't spoken. "What do

you use for fuel? I assume you are using a hybrid fuel that is partially comprised of spent nuclear fuel, since the Americans pay you to dispose of SNF." She frowned. "Of course, the neutronics—you use zirconium hydride moderator rods, correct?—the neutronics are still unfavorable. You would have to add some HEU—High Enrichment Uranium, material from dismantled bombs—to offset it, correct? You put in as much HEU as you can before the plutonium starts coming out of solution, correct?"

At this point Lorenzo and Rhett were just staring at her, mouths hanging slightly open.

"I've dreamed of seeing such reactors," Dash observed wistfully, unaware of the effect she was having on her audience. "How do you get the HEU? I would suppose you would get it from Hanford, but that is far behind the wall around the West Coast Waste. I did not think anyone could go in."

Rhett strode over to join her and Lorenzo at the display. "Ha! You're wrong about that, at least." He paused, and in fairness corrected himself. "Well, you're half right. No one can get into Hanford, though Hanford itself would be perfectly safe to go into if the paranoid bureaucrats would just get out of the way. The missiles didn't reach that far, and there was never really a radiation hazard. But we get our HEU from the North Waste. The survivors living in the Waste bring it south to Inchon, and it's shipped from there."

"Of course," Dash said thoughtfully. "That makes much more sense."

"Well," Rhett said, "perhaps we should let *you* give *us* a tour of *our* facility."

Dash looked puzzled, then realized by looking at everyone's faces that it was a joke. She covered her mouth with her hand as she laughed. "Actually, I was wondering if you could improve your neutronics by supplementing your flux with external solid state neutron generators. Have you seen the latest versions of such generators?" She tapped on her tablet and showed Rhett and Lorenzo a writeup. "With such augmentation, you could use a fuel mix richer in SNF, with less HEU or less fresh five percent LEU. Replacing all the LEU with SNF would mean you could get paid by the American Nuclear Waste Fund for every pound of fuel you use. You could give the power away and still turn a profit."

As Dash started drawing a diagram to show Lorenzo how to position a number of solid state neutron generators around the isle ship's nuclear core, Rhett lifted his eyes and just stared at Colin.

Colin looked back in bemused happiness. "And *that* is why I wanted her here," he said simply. "I'll have to tell Amanda about this one."

"What?" asked Dash distractedly. In the absence of a quick response, she returned to her work on the diagram.

6

A FAMILY MATTER

Perspective is worth 80 IQ points.
  —Alan Kay

Jamal praised Allah once more under his breath. They'd been so close to her this entire time and still couldn't find her. But that time had passed—they owned her now.

Marjan had spotted her coming out of the police station, as he'd surmised, wearing the bright yellow shirt of a peacekeeper. At first he'd been worried that Jameela would spot them, but realized it was unlikely indeed. Who would expect a respectable Pakistani man to be here wearing these outrageous clothes?

The promenade was too crowded for his liking in this final confrontation. A couple witnesses would be acceptable, even desirable given that the video cameras would record his vengeance anyway, unless he could force his way into her cabin. He'd briefly considered breaking into her cabin, but all the walls and doors in this place were solid steel; he couldn't just batter his way in. He had to deal with her elsewhere. Ideally he'd deal with her now, but he'd wait until Jameela moved to someplace a little quieter than the promenade. Then he'd teach her respect.

A young girl wearing glasses and a white lab coat met her with a hearty greeting by a restaurant. The two of them hugged; had Jameela turned to lesbianism? It didn't seem at all farfetched to Jamal, though the other girl seemed a little young for that. Who was she? The only explanation he could come up with was that the girl was the daughter of one of the many doctors here on the *Chiron*, and she was wearing one of her father's coats.

In any event, the girl did not affect his calculations. She was hardly a threat.

Jameela and the girl turned and strode to an elevator. No! He would lose them in the other twenty-five floors of the ship. Jamal rushed to the elevator with no clear plan. Should he kill her right there? No, Marjan was too far away to catch up in time to join him; the confrontation would have to wait.

As Jameela turned to poke the button in the elevator he dodged to the side fast enough, he thought, so she could not see his face.

And then his salvation came. Another woman, already on the elevator, asked Jameela where she wanted to go. And another voice—presumably the young girl's—answered, "Appalachian Spring, please."

The other woman spoke. "Appalachian Spring it is. That's a gorgeous deck, don't you think?" The elevator door slid closed before he heard any response.

Jamal waved Marjan to another elevator which was just opening, and up they went to Appalachian Spring.

They arrived just in time to see a peacekeeper uniform and a white coat turn a corner. Jamal and Marjan ran to meet their destiny.

This was apparently a residential deck. Underneath the admittedly remarkable murals the cabins were dully, monotonously the same, one after the next. They passed a handful of people who watched them in surprise as they rushed by, probably startled to see tourists on this deck.

Jameela and the other girl were laughing as Jamal and Marjan pulled even with them.

Jamal was gasping for breath as he pulled out his *chura*. He'd been too excited about finding her, too afraid of losing her again, and now he was attacking her in a state of weakness. Just like the last time. *Curse the bitch!*

Jameela heard him approach and turned. Her eyes widened as she recognized him, and he watched her eyes follow the knife as he raised it for the downstroke to her chest.

She fell backward at his approach. He howled with glee, excited at seeing her fall before him—until her leg swept up, caught him in the stomach, and assisted him, retaining all his speed and momentum, in sailing down the passage. He crashed badly on the deck. Pain flared in his left shoulder, making him wonder if she'd managed to break something else the way she'd already broken his nose.

He stumbled to his feet, expecting her to be on him before he could get his balance, but she had not pursued him. Instead, she had turned to her brother and proceeded to yell at him as if Jamal himself were unworthy of notice. The young girl in the white coat was sprawled to the side in a daze; presumably Marjan had taken care of her. This seemed particularly likely since Jameela was now stalking toward Marjan, shouting and pointing at the girl on the ground. It seemed momentarily odd to Jamal that she would be so focused on what had happened to the girl when her own death was imminent.

Marjan swung at his sister, but she twisted just enough at the waist to avoid his fist. She kicked him in the knee and he screamed as he stepped back, almost falling when he put weight on the damaged leg.

Enough. Jamal collected himself and rushed back into the fray, this time with his *chura* held forward like a sword. He yelled her name.

Perhaps yelling had been a mistake. At the sound, Jameela glanced back at him, stepped aside, grabbed his knife arm, and pulled him past her.

His knife cut into Marjan's side before he could swerve.

He should have known this would be more difficult than stoning a typical village girl. What had the Pakistani Army been thinking, giving this woman such training?

Jamal bore to the right and swung around until he was on the opposite side of Jameela from Marjan. He howled in rage again, but this time it was part of his strategy.

Jameela turned to face him. This gave Marjan an opportunity to jump forward on his good leg and grab her from behind in a bear hug. Jameela struggled, but her brother was much bigger and stronger. She writhed and swung her head back; the resulting *crack* told Jamal that Marjan's nose was now broken just like his own. But Marjan was obdurate as an ox when it came to rough and tumble. He held on.

Jamal breathed heavily and approached her with satisfaction.

Dash was livid. She felt irritatingly helpless; the bigger of the two thugs had batted her out of the way with an easy swat. She was not one to be discarded so casually.

What could she do? She wished desperately she had her doctor's bag with its very fine scalpel. If she had her scalpel she could show these barbarians some knife work. Alas, she'd left the bag in her lab.

She didn't have any tools to work with...except the pen Dr. Williams had given her during the defense of her experimental plan.

The bigger thug had wrapped his arms around Jam, trapping her for the other one. Could Dash take out the one with the knife? Probably not, but she didn't have to. She was sure Jam, even unarmed, was a better weapon than any knife. She limped swiftly but silently up behind the one holding Jam, jumped on his back, and plunged the tip of her pen into his ear.

Jamal was savoring the moment as he approached his helpless wife. She had stopped struggling, as if resigned to her fate. Though, oddly, there was no evidence of resignation in her eyes. Indeed, she had more of a look of...readiness. Worried, he decided he'd lingered long enough and charged. He thrust his knife forward once more to take her in the chest.

Except at that moment Marjan screamed and twisted. His twist threw off both the aim of Jamal's knife toward Jameela's heart, and Jameela's fierce kick that would have snapped his neck. The knife barely sliced her arm near the shoulder, and the kick missed.

Seconds later Marjan released Jameela. Marjan was still screaming at the top of his lungs. Puzzlingly, he seemed to be wearing the white lab coat. It took Jamal a moment of analysis as Marjan swung this way and that to realize that the young girl had wrapped her legs around his waist. While holding onto him like a rodeo rider on a bronco, she was carefully twisting a black stick buried in the side of his head.

Jamal turned back to Jameela, who had apparently paused a moment to take in the scene as Marjan hopped about. Blood was dripping from her arm in a satisfying way, but the dark rage in her face did not suggest she was incapacitated by it. Rather, it was as if she hadn't yet noticed.

She stalked toward him. He jabbed at her with his knife, but she chopped his wrist and the *chura* fell from his numbed hand. Then she swung at his face.

Not his nose again! He shifted and her fist connected. He felt the pop more than heard it as his jaw broke. He backed away, blinded by pain, holding his hands up to protect himself from another attack as he had done on their last night together.

Jameela leaned over and picked up his *chura*, then walked over to the young girl now sprawled on the ground for a second time. Jameela spoke with her briefly, then turned to Marjan. He was jerking up and down, holding his ear. Jameela smacked him twice in rapid succession to get his attention. She shouted, and he sat down.

Jamal thought it was over, but she glided back to him once more, kicked his legs out from under him, and threw him on his back. She kicked him between the legs. The pain was so great he could not even scream.

She stood over him, hands on her hips. "Divorce me," she demanded.

He stared at her.

She kicked him again. "Divorce me, or I will kick your favorite parts up into your throat."

The girl in the white coat, who was approaching them, cleared her throat. "Technically that is not possible. It is a different system of plumbing."

"I'll manage," Jameela assured her, as she pulled her leg back to encourage him once more.

Jamal opened his mouth to speak. The motion made him jerk, and he would have screamed at the pain from his jaw except that screaming made the pain worse. He leaned forward, pointing at his face, hoping she would wait while he figured out how to make his mouth work. "I divorce you three times," he rasped. Just to make sure she heard, he said it again. "I divorce you three times. I divorce you three times."

Jameela relaxed into a standing position, no longer

threatening him. "Thank you," she said politely. Then she knelt slowly over him, bringing the knife down to his throat. Into his ear she whispered. "If you ever come here again, or send someone else, I shall hunt you. I shall have Dr. Dash here, who is a surgeon, teach me how to castrate pigs. And then, in this as in so much else, you shall be my first. Understood?"

He nodded as vigorously as he could without cutting himself on his own weapon.

Jameela rose so fast, so gracefully, that he couldn't even follow her movement. "What a beautiful day!" she exclaimed.

Then people with yellow shirts started arriving at a run from many directions.

He was going to be doing a lot of explaining to the elders.

Dash still felt like a limp rag as she entered the cafeteria for lunch the next day. Her part in the fight with Jam's ex-husband and Jam's own brother had left her on an adrenalin high that she had enjoyed in a way that still disturbed her. Everyone came to her room and sat on the bed or the sofa listening to her repeat the story of the fight as seen from her perspective. Jam listened quietly, Ping listened eagerly, and Byron listened in horror. Even Colin stopped in for a while, and she had to tell the story once more. When he had left, Dash excused herself from her own party and went to her lab to get some work done while she was still riding the high.

But after the adrenalin came the crash. She'd slept till nearly noon, a flagrant violation of her work ethic. All she wanted to do now was go back to bed, but she squared her shoulders and carried on. She was made of sterner stuff than that. Besides, the mediation for the assault was scheduled for this afternoon. She really needed to eat something beforehand.

After filling her tray with salad and Cajun-style blackened kahala, Dash paused as she looked at her usual table. Byron was already there, arguing with Colin. As she approached, Colin responded. "Yes, we ship anyone who doesn't have a job back where they came from, and that's why there's no poverty here. The BrainTrust is not trying to solve all of the world's problems, Byron."

"We set out to solve one very important problem. We solved it extremely well, I think, and solved an additional number of important problems along the way. But we did not set out to erase all the problems of mankind. Do not expect us to. Many problems remain to be solved by other mobile islands that will take off on new paths in the future, finding new solutions."

Byron snapped, "What problems have you solved other than how to help a lot of really smart people who would have done well anyway get even richer than they would have otherwise gotten?"

Colin snorted. "Well, we solved the healthcare problem, for one."

"What are you talking about? We already solved the healthcare problem in the Blue states. We have universal health coverage. You don't even have that!"

"We do actually, though not for reasons you would

appreciate. But more interestingly, we have healthcare that is responsive, inexpensive, and very high quality." Colin shrugged. "The important problem with healthcare in Western civilization was never choosing which poor schlub should be forced to pay the ridiculously enormous costs. The important issue was always, why is healthcare so overpriced? Here on the BrainTrust we've reduced health-care costs by a factor of ten. Health insurance here is like car insurance dirtside—it's inexpensive enough that no one gets too excited about who foots the bill."

Byron pondered that for a moment, becoming almost calm. "That can't be true. The California government has used its exclusive buying power to clamp down on the pharmaceutical companies and the doctors and the hospitals, forcing them to deliver the lowest possible prices."

Colin shook his head. "Governments are all about punishment. They have no grasp of rewards, except for favored lobbying groups. Here on the BrainTrust we've used simple incentive engineering strategies to reward people who make larger contributions. The consequence is radical innovation in efficiency which ultimately beats the cost savings of governmental clampdown. Focusing on rewards rather than punishments gets better results."

Byron barked a laugh. "So you pay your doctors more to get lower prices."

"Exactly."

Dash added, "Surely you can see how it's done? Consider how we do surgery. A single surgeon typically oversees four simultaneous operations being performed by robots. If the doctor makes half as much money per patient, he is still making twice as much money."

Byron frowned. "That's still only a factor of two savings. Colin is talking about a factor of ten."

Colin picked up the thread. "Excess cost is built into every aspect of American healthcare. In America, an OBGYN pays a hundred thousand a year for liability insurance. On the BrainTrust, mediation practices have reduced that to about five thousand dollars per year, a factor of twenty reduction."

"Still, malpractice insurance is a small part of the total costs."

Colin nodded. "Yes, in America it only costs as much as if you were running a full-blown war in Iraq. But the hidden costs of litigation are a factor of ten greater than that."

Byron shook his head. "Hidden costs?"

"Hidden costs are the ones hardest to control or manage, for obvious reasons. For example, doctors do relentless testing, all too often not to protect the patient from the illness or side effects but to protect the doctor from the litigation." Colin peered into a distant memory. "Once, long ago, I had pleurisy, an irritation in the lining of the lungs. When it flared in the middle of the night, I went to the emergency room to make sure it hadn't turned into pneumonia, as my doctor had warned me to do. Twenty seconds with a stethoscope showed it wasn't a problem, but the doctor ran an MRI to make sure I wasn't having a heart attack. He knew I wasn't, but he had to protect himself and his hospital. That compulsion turned what should have been a twenty-five-dollar doctor visit into a three-thousand-dollar nightmare."

Dash did the calculation. "So in this example the

liability issues inflated the costs by more than a factor of one hundred."

Colin nodded and continued, "And of course, doctors from all over the world compete for the opportunity to work here, some on board the ships, some remotely. We have some Canadian doctors, whose salaries were fixed by the government as you noted, who moved to Bermuda, work from the beach, and make more money than ever before by offering a lower price per patient than the doctors in competition with them."

Byron snorted. "They can't possibly provide the best quality care."

Colin shrugged. "If they don't give excellent care, they don't get any more patients. I said earlier we focus on rewards for excellence, but we do have a stick, too. In America, the medical industry never allows more doctors to be certified than there are patients to serve the doctors' need for full schedules. On the BrainTrust, the competition among doctors worldwide to serve the patients' needs is nothing short of ferocious. Any medical practitioner who puts people in waiting lines or delivers poor service is swept from the field."

Dash added, "Like the MRI machine we just purchased for the lab. Remember, Byron? The MRI that passed the American FDA certification process was quoted at a hundred thousand dollars, so we bought the one from India that cost ten thousand dollars. Another factor of ten, now that I think about it."

"Bah!" Byron changed the topic, though not as much as Dash might have preferred. "I was wondering, Dash, if you had thought any more about what I said about the moral issues with your therapy."

"You mean treating tyrants and dictators?" Dash shook her head. "I will say again, it would be most unwise of them to want to be part of our current research."

Byron pressed. "But if they did?" He turned to Colin. "Has anyone in the President's office contacted you?"

When Colin failed to respond promptly, Dash looked at him in surprise. "*Pak* Colin, does the President-for-Life want to be an experimental patient?"

Colin frowned. "It was discussed. In the end his people rejected the idea."

"See!?" Byron demanded. "They're already hounding you, and it'll just get worse."

Dash closed her eyes for a moment. "So you want me to create rules about who will be allowed to receive telomere therapy? I should pick who lives and who dies?" She shook her head. "I just do not see it, Byron. People will have to find a more sensible way of replacing national leaders than waiting for them to die."

Byron slid forward in his chair and challenged her. "Like what?"

Dash lowered her head. "I do not know." She raised her eyes to meet his. "But as *Pak* Colin said earlier, we are not trying to solve all of the world's problems. You and I have set out to solve one very important problem. I think we may solve it pretty well, but many other problems will remain. And this problem—the immortal dictator problem —is outside my areas of expertise." Though as she thought about it, she wondered if maybe she should expand her horizons. Perhaps she should *make* it an area of expertise.

Byron rose abruptly from the table and stalked away, practically shaking with anger.

Colin watched him sadly. "If he's not careful, he'll wind up a bitter old man."

Dash defended her assistant, at least a little. "His question is still interesting. Furthermore, it is about to become much more important. How might we make the process for replacing a bad dictator more reliable?"

Colin stared at her thoughtfully. "To get a better answer, you need to ask a better question." He too rose from the table and left.

And Dash sat nibbling on her kahala, pondering the question of what question she should ask.

———

Mediator Joshua Pickett was astonished. Two cases of violent assault on security personnel in such a short period of time. Extraordinary! And both assaults had taken place here on his ship, the *Chiron*. Coincidence, or were they somehow connected?

Scanning the brief documents on the assailants, it struck him that these two, like the first one, were from Pakistan. Indeed, looking more closely at his data, he saw that the previous accused, one of these two, and the peacekeeper at the center of this latest incident all had the same last name. The probability of a coincidence seemed small indeed.

Well, on to the facts.

He faced a larger group of people this time, but some of the faces were the same. "Amanda?"

Amanda nodded graciously. "As it happens, I know the peacekeeper and the resident involved. Dr. Dash is a research lead here on *Chiron*. Although she is project owner for an independent venture-sponsored startup, I am part of the technical team reviewing her work on behalf of the investors."

Joshua pursed his lips. "Colin."

Amanda just shrugged.

He looked beyond her. "Ms. Ping?"

"Just Ping, sir. Dash and Jam are friends of mine. I'm here for moral support."

Joshua wondered if she was really here in hopes that another fight would break out so she'd be able to participate. Well, considering how violence-wracked the ship had suddenly become, perhaps her presence was not a bad thing.

He next turned to one of the assaulted parties. "Dr. Dash?"

"Yes, sir. If you need an assessment of the medical condition of the participants here, I would be happy to assist."

"I suspect Amanda, that is, Dr. Copeland, can fill that capacity for today. You've had a rather rough couple of hours. But thank you." He turned to the peacekeeper standing next to her. "Mrs. Yousafzai?"

Jam stood stiffly at attention. "I am no longer Mrs. Yousafzai, sir. After the altercation, I persuaded my husband to divorce me. It is done. Please call me Jam."

"Jam." Joshua made a notation for the record. "I presume your, erm, ex-husband is Mr. Jamal Yousafzai?"

He looked over at the man whose jaw was locked in position by external wiring.

A BrainTrust guest advocate was standing next to him. "Excuse me, sir, but as you can see, Mr. Yousafzai is not able to speak on his own behalf. I shall be acting as his voice as well as his counsel."

"Very good. He turned to the last man. "Can you speak for yourself, Mr., uh, Tarkani?"

Marjan answered through his phone translator. "Yes, sir." His voice sounded a bit muffled; Joshua realized his nose was broken and packed with cotton. The nose had been a victim of the battle, Joshua guessed. Interesting that Jamal's nose appeared to have been broken in the same way some time in the past—unless that was a common nose shape among Pakistani men. Rather unlikely, he supposed.

"Everyone, please be seated." They all sat, except the four peacekeepers standing behind Jamal and Marjan. They seemed disturbingly alert for any transgression on the part of the guests that might give them an opportunity to dispense more justice. Joshua shook his head. "Let's see what happened, shall we?"

There were so many vidcams in the vicinity of this assault that they could construct a 3D composite. He observed the moment when Marjan's nose suffered its fate. He paused toward the end, when Jamal was lying on the ground turning purple after Jam kicked him in a most sensitive area. "Ms. Jam. I fear I have to ask. Is this the point at which you renegotiated your marital arrangement with your ex-husband?"

Jam stared forward. "It is, sir."

Joshua spoke forcefully. "You understand that it is inappropriate for a representative of the BrainTrust, an autonomous society which strives to represent the highest standards of civilization, to negotiate with a tourist in this fashion?"

Jam's eyes glistened. "I am sorry, sir. I was not thinking clearly at the time. I had lost sight of the fact that he was a guest."

Joshua buried his head in his hands. He muttered his mantra to himself once again, "This is not funny. This is a serious matter," and placed his hands calmly on the desk. "Please strive to do better in the future, Ms. Jam."

"Yes, sir."

The video ended.

Joshua looked at Jamal. "It would seem you were attempting to murder our peacekeeper."

Jamal turned to the advocate and whispered something slowly. The advocate spoke for him. "He says he was simply attempting to restore his family's honor, sir. He begs forgiveness and prays for understanding."

Joshua turned to Jam. "Does that mean he was not trying to kill you?"

"It means that a year ago I broke his nose to escape a beating, sir. He will remain disgraced as long as I live." She reached up involuntarily and touched the scar below her eye.

The scar looked remarkably similar to the scar that had been forming on Amu's face when Joshua had last seen him. He looked at Ping, who grinned back. He was suddenly certain that justice was being served in ways he would be better off not investigating. "Ms. Jam, Dr. Dash, do you have any serious injuries to report? I see your arm is taped up, Ms. Jam, presumably from that knife slash we witnessed on the video?"

Jam shook her head, "I am fine, sir."

Dash raised her hand to speak. "I am fine, but I feel obligated to note another injury Jam has suffered. In contact with her attacking ex-husband, she experienced severe abrasions to the joints of her hand."

Joshua took a few seconds to parse this sentence. He rolled the video to the place where he suspected the injury had taken place. "Was this the point at which Ms. Jam suffered these abrasions?"

Dash looked at him very seriously. "Yes."

Joshua rolled his lips. "You're telling me that Ms. Jam hurt her knuckles when she broke Mr. Yousafzai's jaw?"

Dash seemed set on arguing, then reconsidered. "It was a very serious abrasion."

Joshua put his head in his hands again and silently ran his mantra through his mind. Three times. "Of course." He looked at Jamal and Marjan.

"What about the injuries to our two other participants?"

Amanda answered. "The broken jaw looks bad, but it will heal nicely. We recommend holding them on board till we can remove the bracing."

"And Mr. Tarkani?"

Dash answered this time. "The damage to his eardrum is minor."

Marjan turned stiffly. "What?" he asked.

"Though the hearing loss is considerable," Dash continued smoothly.

The advocate felt obligated to object. "Mediator Pickett, allow me to point out that my client cannot see very well because the pain of his broken nose causes tears to well in his eyes, and he cannot hear very well because of the damage to his eardrum. I hardly think the damage is minor."

Dash could not let that stand. "I assure you the damage is minor. I was very careful to penetrate the ear with the pen in such a manner as to fully distract Mr. Tarkani while inflicting as little damage as possible."

Joshua was incredulous. "So, in the middle of a desperate fight with assailants intent on murdering your friend, you were *careful* while jamming a pen into the assailant's ear?"

"Of course," Dash responded primly.

Joshua was about to ream her out for claims perilously close to perjury when Amanda coughed politely. He turned to her.

"Josh—I mean, Mediator Pickett—speaking as a friend of the mediation, I'm quite certain she's telling the truth. 'First do no harm,' you know."

Dash interjected, "Very much so. I take my oath seriously."

Amanda continued. "That's just the way she is. Really." Her expression turned rueful.

Joshua looked between the two of them. "Well, then."

Dash looked a little guilty. "A surgeon of even mediocre skill could repair his eardrum. I can fix it if you want me to." She paused. The next words seemed forced from her. "The nose, too."

Amanda glared at her, though Dash seemed oblivious. Joshua addressed Amanda. "Dr. Copeland? You have something you wish to add?"

Amanda spoke with barely controlled fury. "We are already fulfilling our contractual obligation to these attempted murderers. We do not need to go to any such extremes."

Joshua was inclined to agree. "Very well."

A wicked smile lit Jam's face.

Joshua knew it would be better if he did not pursue this, but chose the course of unwisdom. "Ms. Jam, do you have something to add?"

Jam stared at her brother. "The doctor in our village is a butcher. Many women have died during childbirth because of his incompetence. Handing Marjan over to him for surgery would be…" she groped for the right words, "an act of justice."

Ah, yes. Justice. A goal ever to strive for, never to achieve. Joshua wondered how well he was doing here today. Were he striving to serve irony rather than justice, he thought he would be doing rather well. "We'll hold Mr. Tarkani and Mr. Yousafzai until the broken jaw is healed enough for transport. Then they'll be shipped back to Pakistan."

Amanda objected. "Joshua, these people are murderers! An honor killing? You know what'll happen to them if we just send them back. They'll just be sent home with no jail time and no punishment." She calmed down. "Sir."

Joshua waved his hands helplessly. "What else can I do?" He looked at the battered pair of men. He thought of the three wise monkeys: See no evil, hear no evil, speak no evil. Between the two of them, they had all the injuries needed to be wise. "Perhaps they have already received a minimally educational set of punishments from their intended victims." He was about to end the meeting when Jamal spoke urgently to the advocate. The advocate delivered Jamal's request. "Uh, sir, Mr. Yousafzai would like to have his knife returned to him when he departs."

"The knife?" he asked in puzzlement.

"Yes." The advocate gestured to one of the security guards, who brought forth the item in question.

"Ah." Suddenly Joshua had a thought. "Is this knife valuable?"

Jamal nodded his head vigorously. He spoke to the advocate. The advocate spoke back. Jamal spoke angrily. The advocate countered in frustration. Still more words. Finally the advocate relented. Joshua realized the advocate'd had the same thought as himself, but Jamal wasn't listening.

The advocate spoke with resignation. "The knife is very valuable, and it's a family heirloom." He looked down at his feet sadly. "It's very important to him."

Joshua smiled in satisfaction. "How wonderful." He addressed Jamal and Marjan. "You know, normally in mediation, the conflict comes down to money. The injured party receives compensatory remuneration for damages. We didn't discuss such remuneration during this mediation because you two don't have a dime between the pair of you." Here he smiled, "but compensation need not be financial. I hereby transfer ownership of the knife." He looked at it closely. "An ivory-hilted knife with a curved blade—"

Jam interrupted. "A *chura*."

"Excellent. I hereby transfer ownership of this *chura* to

Dr. Dash and Ms. Jam." He looked at them. "You'll have to figure out a way to share it."

Jam shook her head. "I don't want it. Dash, it's yours."

Dash looked bemused. "What would I do with it?"

Ping shouldered her way between the two of them. "Give it to me," she chirped. "I mean, really, I'm the only one of the three of us who has a clue how to use a knife like this."

Dash went to the mediator's table, took the knife, and handed it to Ping.

Jamal was dragged from the room howling for his property.

The next day Dash awoke slowly as pseudo-daylight filtered into her room from her virtual balcony, a very fancy cruise liner-esque name for the immense screen covering half a wall that replayed the real-time view of the ocean just beyond the *Elysian Fields*.

Normally at this time of day that patch of ocean was empty. Later the area would fill with jet skis and windsurfers, but dawn was quiet. Today, however, a major laser tag game was being held, and it had started the moment the sun popped above the horizon.

Dash found the laser tag players quite entertaining. Ping had told her that normally laser tag was played by individuals with pistols, ducking and dodging across an obstacle field. Ping had urged her to play a round, so that, as Ping explained, "I can nail your sorry ass." Given that incentive, Dash had demurred.

The virtual balcony was showing her the BrainTrust version of laser tag, played with copters buzzing each other across the water. When a laser tagger scored a hit on another copter, the downed flyer automatically lost his guns and had to return to the floating helicopter pad.

The copters were all home-brewed designs. One looked like a flying saucer with six holes around the outer edge for the turbofans. Another had an octagon of spindly poles arcing out from a central chair just large enough for the pilot. Dash thought the best one looked like the Jetsons' skycar, and it moved with a speed the others must have envied.

Copter tech had evolved at revolutionary speed on the BrainTrust because of the low costs and simple certification processes. You could fly any wacky design-prototype copter in the laser tag competition as long as you didn't fly over the isle ships and kept the altitude within thirty feet of the sea's surface. A thousand hours of accident-free operation by five or more pilots, and the restrictions were lifted.

A number of venture capitalists, Colin had explained, were avid watchers of the battles. Several copter designs had been licensed and were now manufactured dirtside, though none of them were made or flown in America or Europe. "Too dangerous," the regulatory wise men of Western civilization universally agreed. "Too fat a litigation target," the investors responded instinctively. That was why America still didn't have flying cars. At least that was what Colin had said, though he might have been trying to get a rise out of Byron at the time.

Music wafted in from the passage. Beautiful music.

Music? Dash struggled to her feet and pulled a Balinese

sarung around herself as she listened. It was a woman's voice, singing a melody with no words. She thought she recognized the music, and smiled as she realized it was Aaron Copland's *Appalachian Spring*. She had looked it up after finding out she would be living on the Appalachian Spring deck.

The voice was remarkable, even through the walls of her cabin. She was even more amazed that this lone voice could carry a tune designed for a symphony. She swung open her door.

Jam stood in the middle of the passage, eyes closed, face raised to the sky in the deck's artificial dawn.

Movement on her right made her look to the side, and she saw Ping step hesitantly beyond her door. Ping began to sing, backing up Jam's alto with a remarkable soprano.

Another door on the passage quietly opened. And another.

A bicyclist rolling down the hall slowed to a stop.

People started to arrive and sit or stand in the passage. The neighbors must have called friends who were singers, because a remarkable percentage of the new arrivals joined in. Soon it was a symphony indeed.

Dash noticed another odd thing—there were no cell phones in the air recording the event. Unplanned, this had become a private concert, an ephemeral moment that would exist only in the memories of the people here.

She remembered a writeup she had seen about the origins of the music. Copland had written it for a woman who had, he explained, "Something prim and restrained, a strong quality about her, that one tends to think of as American."

In Copland's era, Dash realized, Jam would have made an excellent American. Today, she was perfect as a member of the BrainTrust.

Dash leaned against her cabin door, closed her eyes, and simply listened.

7

EXPERIMENTS IN AGING

Just imagine how much happier you would be if a prematurely deceased loved one were alive, or a debilitated one were vigorous —and multiply that good by several billion, in perpetuity. Given this potential bonanza, the primary moral goal for today's bioethics can be summarized in a single sentence. Get out of the way.

—Steven Pinker, "Boston Globe, A Moral Imperative for Bioethics"

She gave her patients their customized primary injections, and for three days and three nights everything went as planned. Which was to say, nothing happened as the telomere replicators distributed themselves throughout the bodies of the patients.

On the morning of the fourth day Dash slumped exhausted over her desk, her head cradled in her arms. She heard heavy, fast footsteps come through the door. She did not look up. "What, Byron?"

"News." He hesitated. "Good and bad. The replicators are having an effect." Another pause. "Many different effects, actually."

Dash opened her eyes slowly, rolling her head as she straightened her back and stretched. "Let us see."

The nearest patient was Randa. She was snoring lightly. When Dash entered the room, her husband looked up and nodded silently.

Dash studied the charts on the digital displays around the room as she muttered, "Pipelines."

Randa looked up at the sound. She smiled. "Is that how you remember me? As the pipeline girl?"

Dash smiled in return. "Not any more. You are no longer the pipeline girl. You are the girl who lived." She studied the screens for another moment. "Ten years, I estimate, by many measures of age." She looked sternly at the elderly woman. "However, you are not younger. This is not a Fountain of Youth. But..." she reluctantly continued, "based on the progress being made by reinvigorated cell divisions and replacements, you would not be entirely off in your assessment if you concluded you felt ten years younger a month from now."

Randa clapped, laughed, and touched her face. "What about all these wrinkles?"

Dash shook her head. "I suspect that ten years ago you already had those laugh lines. You will have to live with them."

Her husband spoke for the first time. "Her laugh lines

are what make her beautiful. She'll definitely have to live with them."

Randa looked at him with wonder. "I suppose I shall."

───────

Byron spoke as they walked the short distance to Ben Wilson's room. "Mr. Wilson has had the oddest reaction of anyone."

"Yes?"

"None at all."

"Interesting." Dash entered Ben's room, finding that his grandson had pulled sentry duty for the moment. The two of them were speaking quietly when she interrupted. "Mr. Wilson, good morning."

He frowned at her. "I told you to call me Ben."

"Very well, Ben." Dash studied his charts for a brief moment. "Well, Ben, you are an interesting case."

Ben closed his eyes and shuddered. "Oh, no. I learned long ago that being an interesting case was bad news."

His grandson reached out and took his hand. "It's ok, Papa."

Dash shook her head from side to side. "There is good news. The telomere replicators did not harm you."

"And?"

"They also did not lengthen any of your telomere chains." She leaned over and peered at one line on the nearest screen. "They seem to have entered the cells of your body, but they never engaged with your chromosomes, and now they have all been flushed out of your system. I have no idea what happened." She pursed her lips.

Ben laughed, a thin edge of hysteria in the sound. "Well, if you had wanted me to continue funding you, this outcome would probably work."

Dash frowned.

He waved his hand. "Joking, just joking. I would have continued to fund you regardless." He shook his head. "Unless I died, of course, in which case you would definitely need other funding." He shook his finger at her, raising his eyebrow in a mocking expression. "I would still fund you even if I were a corpse, you understand, if it were allowed."

"I'm sorry it did not work."

"That's why they call it an experimental procedure, Dr. Dash." Their eyes met for a moment. "If you figure out what went wrong and need another test subject, you'll think of me first, won't you?" He was very serious.

She touched his shoulder. "Count on it."

They found Carl bent over a pad of old-fashioned paper, scribbling furiously with a traditional pencil. He looked at his tablet from time to time, making modifications to a simulation program.

Dash watched him for a couple of minutes, averse to interrupting him. Finally he looked up. "My head hurts." He winced. "It really hurts." He went back to scribbling.

Dash looked around at the displays. A look of alarm spread over her face. "This is very bad."

Byron raised an eyebrow, and she pointed. He answered his own question. "The replicators are overstimulating the neurons throughout the cranium." He looked at her again. "How can that be?"

Dash shook her head.

Carl moaned. As he paused for a moment the left hand, the one holding the pencil, started shaking. He grasped his left hand in his right, and slowly, painfully, went back to his work.

Dash touched his wrist. "Carl."

He looked up. "I almost have it. I'm really close." He ripped the page from the pad, and held it up to her. "Can you see?"

Dash studied the page. "Almost." She ran a finger under one passage in one equation. "What's this?"

"It's…it's…self-evident." He looked into her eyes. "What's happening to me?"

Dash glanced at the monitors. It was too painful to her to maintain eye contact. "The replicators are no longer following their expected behavior." She exhaled. "While all your neurons are firing at unexpected intervals, the ones that process the sensation of pain are the worst." She thought of an analogy. "You know how you can set the timing circuit on a computer chip to fire faster, running the chip at a higher speed until it overheats and fails?"

Carl nodded. "Overclocking."

"Think of it as overclocking in your mind." A very painful form of overclocking. And it was accelerating.

"That explains it. Aspects of my formula that I couldn't understand before are now clear. I just have to get them down on paper." He started writing again, but the scrawl was illegible.

Dash tapped on a keyboard and a pale pink chemical

slid into the IV line attached to his wrist. "This may help with the pain, at least a little bit. For a little while." She shook her head. "But the source of the pain is actually inside your brain."

"And you cannot shut it off without shutting me off. I understand." He continued to write, and in a few moments the numbers and symbols became legible again. "I-I don't think I will make it." He looked up at her and feverishly grabbed her arm. She stood passively. "You understand. Will you finish it for me?"

She looked at the equations again. She had a sense that there were a couple of things that could be, should be improved upon, and it would make a difference. "You work on it more it first. I will take it from there."

He laid back in the bed, his muscles relaxing for the first time. His eyes closed. "I'll go back to it in a minute."

Dash turned to Byron. "Stay with him."

Byron nodded. "I'll make sure he gets some sleep."

Dash thought about it for a moment, then shook her head. "Help him stay awake. He has little time. Enable him to make the most of it."

Ryan was kicking his covers and screaming when Dash walked in. A nurse turned to her and said, "I was about to call you. The pain meds aren't working."

Dash nodded. "It is not normal pain. She tapped on the machines, and a dose of the same light pink medication as Carl's moved down the tube to his wrist.

Ryan stopped kicking. "I don't suppose that's a symptom of healing."

"I'm sorry."

"You have to fix it!" he shouted, then kicked again and grabbed at her. Dash stepped back, reaching for the call button.

"No, don't get the goons." His whole body arched in some combination of pain and misery and collapsed nerveless onto the bed. "It's over then, huh?"

Dash considered for a moment. "Shall I call your relatives?"

He chuckled. "That crew? I've repaired many votes in my time, but today if they had to vote, I'd probably already be dead."

"Do not underestimate them."

More chuckling greeted her. "Trust me, underestimating is not in my character." A new surge of pain transfixed his face. "Is that the best painkiller you've got?"

"I have nothing better."

"Where's the button to finish it?"

Dash pointed mutely at a toggle by his side, nestled under a snap cover.

"I just open the cover, flip the toggle?"

"And press this button." Dash pointed at the last control on the instrument.

"Fine." He flipped the cover off. "Ok, you can call in the cannibals now."

Dash nodded to the nurse, who started briskly for the door. "Tell them to hurry," Dash called after her.

"Don't you have other patients to attend to? Get out."

She bowed to him, then took her leave as he pressed the final button.

Dash stood in the hallway gathering herself for a moment. Cries came from Ryan's room, and an elderly woman came out. "Bet he gave you a very hard time in the end."

Dash almost smiled. "Yes."

"Good. He was happy then." The woman patted her cheek. "I'll tell everyone what happened. You go on."

A gurney was already being wheeled toward them. "Thank you," Dash answered.

She walked to Lucas' room. She shuddered a moment, then straightened her back and entered.

Lucas turned from his sister as he heard her. "Good morning," he offered.

Dash felt overwhelmed with relief. "Good morning," she replied, with perhaps an excess of enthusiasm. Was she gushing? Unacceptable.

Dash strolled around, studying the monitors.

"How is it, Doc?"

"Fifteen years, Mr. Kahn." She looked at him sternly. "It is not rejuvenation, of course. But you may have fifteen more years now than you had before. We'll see in the course of the next thirty days, but that is my best estimate at this time."

Lucas' sister closed her eyes; tears welled from underneath the lids.

Lucas smacked his hand on the rail of the bed, creating

an unimpressive dull thud. "Hah! Now I'm younger than you, Trini!"

She opened her eyes; they danced with laughter. "You've always been younger than me, Lucas. You've always been a spoiled three-year-old."

Dash shook her head. "Please do not get too frisky yet. As I said, this is a preliminary estimate." She glanced at a clock on one of the monitors. "I must go," she said, and departed.

She walked briskly toward Tom's room, elated with Lucas' response to treatment. She had two successes! She had hoped for this, but she had forced herself to remain skeptical. The failures seemed less terrible.

Her pace faltered as she came around a corner and saw Byron hustling into a room, accompanied by two nurses. Tom's room.

In the moments it took her to reach them, it was over. Byron looked up at her. "At least this one was sudden. As in, virtually instantaneous." He waved his hands around at the monitors. "You can see for yourself, but as nearly as I can tell, the membranes on his neurons started to dissolve and the cells more or less exploded." He shook his head. "It'll take some time to figure out what happened."

Dash looked at the monitors briefly, then decided she would analyze the data another day. "Go back and check on Carl. I will take a break, then go see Anne." Byron hustled off, and Dash moved more slowly toward the floor's small café.

The Voice of the Silent watched in delight as four gun barrels formed in the printer's well, one layer of sintered titanium powder at a time.

Drew, Jerry, and Chuck looked at Howie, who had rented the printer, in amazement. Drew asked the necessary questions, rattling like a machine gun himself. "How did you know to do this? Why aren't the cops crawling around us yet? Where'd you get the plans? Will this work like a real gun?"

Howie drew his eyes away from the miracle forming in the machine that was his new best friend. "First of all, it won't just work like a real gun—it'll work better, at least for the duration of our trip. These are top-of-the-line 3D printers here, guys. The BrainTrust uses them to manufacture parts for the next generation of isle ships." The Voice of the Silent had been given a printer near the window when they asked for a couple of hours of rental time, and Howie pointed outside at the more-than-half-built isle ship taking shape next door. "We're gonna have guns made out of frickin' titanium! Fifty thousand a pop, if you bought one in Texas! These're better than my Winchester back home." He slapped Drew on the back. "As for why the cops haven't shown up yet, we aren't makin' guns here. We're just makin' parts for a homebrew copter. You know, the laser tag." He pointed at the gun barrels, now large enough you could see their shape. "Those aren't gun barrels, Drew. Those're just tubes for a part of the fuel lines to the vertical props."

Chuck shook his head in awe. "And thus God uses the wicked to lift up the righteous."

Drew was still a little baffled. "Ok, but how'd you get the plans? The Web, I guess?"

Howie nodded. "Yeah, these are plans that intentionally break the rifle down into a series of separate print runs that're almost impossible to recognize as rifle parts. And I knew from the BrainTrust website that we could rent the printers. Everybody rents time on these things: copter inventors, engineering startup companies, and the kids at the university, of course, for their lab projects." His expression turned wistful. "If these printers didn't cost ten mil apiece, we could make a fortune back home printing every kind of weapon and tool needed to do God's work during Armageddon."

Jerry asked the obvious logistical question. "Cartridges?"

Howie shook his head. "The bullets themselves would be easy, but the primers for the propellants would be impossible. You remember how I hobbled aboard with two canes?"

Everyone nodded.

"Well, the canes were full of ammo packed in paraffin."

Jerry clapped Howie on the shoulder. "Howie, it was God's will that you should find us and we should find you just in time to make the trip."

"Amen," agreed Drew and Chuck.

As they packed the gun barrels, a number of small parts started to take shape in the next run. Jerry figured it out first. "That's like half a firing mechanism, those pieces tabbed together in odd shapes? We'll have to file the tabs off."

Howie grinned. "It's good to be workin' with such smart folk."

Jerry turned to Chuck. "How're we doin' on gettin' the fertilizer?"

Chuck shrugged. "Every day there's a shipment from the *Hephaestus*, where they manufacture it. They move it in smallish quantities on a daily basis because—get this— they think it's dangerous." That got a grin from everyone. McVeigh had knocked down a Fed building decades earlier using this same kind of fertilizer. "We have a fellow believer on the cargo deck wrangling bots. If I'm lucky, I should be able to snag a couple fifty-pound cans." He suspected that his wrangler friend would be happy enough to help if he heard the whole story, but Jack would be better off knowing nothing, so Chuck planned to use a bit of legerdemain to make it look like the cans were lost overboard during the transfer. It was the weakest part of the whole plan, but God would see him through.

Drew laughed suddenly. "This whole plan is goin' so smooth, it's like shootin' deer from a helicopter."

"With titanium guns," agreed Howie.

"God's will," Chuck chimed in.

"Amen," said Jerry.

For a long time, Dash sat in the café sipping a cup of white tea. She had no idea what she would find when she went into Anne's room, but she wasn't ready for it even if it was good news.

Byron slipped into the chair next to her. His eyes looked dark, and he clutched a sheaf of papers tightly.

She stared at the papers. "He's gone," she whispered.

He held out the papers. "For you."

She leafed through the pages, barely comprehending them, but seeing enough. "It's not yet done." The formulas and equations pressed on her eyeballs, trying to get in, to be seen, to be understood, to be appreciated. She dared not do it.

There was just too much.

Colin's words echoed in her head. *We set out to solve one very important problem. We solved it extremely well, I think, and solved a number of additional important problems along the way. But we did not set out to erase all the problems of mankind. Do not expect us to.*

Dash had a single problem to solve. She had not solved it yet, but she would, along with several others. But not this one.

She would digitize the papers and publish them as they were. Perhaps one day she would find someone to pass them on to. Someone to appreciate them as they deserved.

She felt a burden lift from her heart. Having determined her plan, she allowed the symbols to leak into her mind. She made a few notations—questions, really—in the margins. Just jotting down thoughts that might be interesting to consider, she went on and on, until she had no more. Then she was ready to go back to the problem she would solve.

One of Anne's daughters had paid an enormous

premium for an enormous room to allow her entire family to sit with her. She was sitting up in bed, and when she looked at Dash, she smiled in alert recognition. "Dr. Dash. It's so good to see you."

Dash stood gaping at her. Was this the same woman who could barely focus her eyes the last time they'd met, who had thought Dash was one of the refugees she had assisted twenty years earlier? "Ms. Rainer."

"Call me Anne," the matriarch demanded.

"Anne. You seem to have made an extraordinary recovery." Dash walked amongst the monitors again, marveling at the story they told.

Anne gave her a few moments to study the displays, then interrupted her assessment with a peremptory word. "So, am I ready to run a marathon yet? I certainly feel like it." She started to rise from the bed, but the wires and tubes got in her way. "You really must let me up," she asserted. "It's very hard to play bridge with my daughters while sitting in a bed. We need a table." She nodded at one of her great-granddaughters. "And Nora wants to serve a proper tea. A hospital bed is simply not a suitable accommodation."

Dash just shook her head. "Let me call a nurse." She moved toward the controls, but a red line of data awakened on the screen.

"Aaah," Anne moaned, then sank back onto the bed. "Argh. Too much, I guess."

Dash watched the numbers on the screen, and her joyous smile slowly warped into a grimace. "It is not you, I am afraid, Anne." She hissed softly. "Lie back. Enjoy your family. Let them enjoy you."

Anne nodded. "I'm on a short clock, then."

Dash lowered her eyes. She started a slow drip of pain meds and went outside to wait.

At first she let the sound of the hushed laughter emanating from the room wash over her, but too soon that faded. After that, she caught the occasional urgent whispers of matters too sensitive to allow the children in the room to hear.

A shoe scuffed on the floor next to her, and she looked up to see Nora looking at her, wide-eyed. "Dr. Dash, Gran wants to see you."

Once more, Dash straightened her back and walked into the valley of death.

Anne's relatives walked passed her single file, shaking her hand and thanking her for her efforts. Dash could not speak; she had no words rich enough to express her grief. Finally she was alone with Anne, whose face was now set in a rictus of pain. But there was still a little laughter in her eyes, eyes that were sharp and clear. She shifted on the bed and struggled with the euthanasia toggle as her hands shook. "This is harder than it ought to be," Anne muttered softly.

Dash went to the side of the bed. "I can help you, to some extent." She opened the safety and flipped the toggle.

"Would you push the button for me, please?" Anne asked.

"You must do that yourself." Dash felt tears shimmering as her vision blurred. "I'm so sorry I could not save you."

Anne shook her head. "Don't you understand? Yesterday I was drooling, and couldn't recognize my own son. Today I taught my great granddaughter an important life lesson: though your performance may not go as well as you hoped, you can always finish with grace and charm." She reached out, grabbed Dash's wrist, and gave her a shake. "Do not worry about saving me. You already did." She released her handhold, and with a last fluid motion, she stabbed the button.

Moments later she exhaled, and her spirit rode away with her breath.

Dash did not—quite—run from the room, down the corridor, up the stairway, and out into the open, into the tang of the ocean breeze.

Dash was not quite sure how her friends had found her, or how they'd known they were needed. Nevertheless, she'd been happy when they had come up to her and silently given her a joint hug.

When she was depressed, one of her defenses was to plunge into learning something new. One bit of historical education had been taunting her for a while. So Dash led her friends down into the bowels of *GPlex I* until they reached the entrance to her destination. Bowing to her friends and pointing the way, she said with satisfaction, "Here we are."

Ping stared at the sign, a slab of dull gray concrete inlaid with silvery-metallic lettering. **Museum of Ocean Autonomy**. She groaned.

Dash laughed lightly; it felt good to be happy for a moment. "You do not have to come in if you do not desire."

Ping looked at her hopefully. Jam nudged her hard with

a hip. A bright, though rigid, smile appeared on Ping's face. "No, I'd love to see all the…ancient history."

"Good." Dash grabbed Ping's arm and hauled her inside. Ping looked sideways at Jam and stuck a finger in her own mouth to indicate gagging. Jam gave a melodious laugh.

The first thing they came to, right inside the entrance, was a large model of a ship encased in glass. Ping complained, "That's just a cruise liner. What's the big deal?"

Dash frowned. "Even if she were 'just a cruise liner,' it would be a worthy exhibit. Cruise liners could reasonably be described as the first semi-autonomous floating cities. Particularly the later ones, which carried up to ten thousand people. But she is not actually a cruise liner. This is *The World*, the first semi-autonomous residential ship."

"Ooookay. It still looks like a cruise ship."

Dash growled briefly, though her growl sounded more like a puppy than a Doberman. "Ships are 'she,' not 'it.' In 2006, *The World's* owners sold all her cabins to permanent homeowners. While many of the homeowners only lived on board part-time, many of them were permanent. The ship's routes and destinations were chosen by the residents."

Jam raised an eyebrow. "The cabins must have been expensive."

"Oh, yes. Much more expensive than the cabins on normal cruise liners of the time, which cost about as much per square foot as a New York apartment. But the owners of *The World* were able to charge a remarkable premium due to the exclusivity. To be considered to purchase a cabin, you had to have at least ten million dollars in assets."

Ping said, "Well, that sounds like a lot, but there are lots of people with that much money."

"And you had to be invited to submit a request by an existing homeowner."

Jam offered. "So you had to be nice to someone."

"And then all the existing homeowners had to vote you in."

Silence ruled for a moment. Ping admitted, "I guess it *was* pretty exclusive, at that."

Jam asked, "Why was it called semi-autonomous? The captain had final authority over everything, didn't he, like most ships?"

Dash reflected on that for a moment. Suddenly she understood why Colin had described the BrainTrust as a corporate dictatorship. All ships were, at the end of the day, very nearly dictatorships when they were at sea, ruled solely by their captains. *The World* was only semi-autonomous because it had to put in to harbor frequently for food and fuel."

In contrast, BrainTrust isle ships did not put into any port. The BrainTrust Consortium, to whom each isle ship captain reported, for all intents and purposes maintained continuous rule. At the end of the day, if you didn't like the way the BrainTrust operated, your only recourse was to leave. Which, Dash reflected, was actually a very powerful check on the power of the Consortium. The Consortium desperately needed the best and brightest aboard the ships, else the Consortium would quickly find itself penniless and broken.

Remembering something she'd read before embarking

on her voyage, she muttered, "A choice is better than a voice."

Ping leaned over to hear better. "What was that?"

Dash shook her head. "Just an old quote from some of the people who did the early work preparing the way for the building of the BrainTrust."

As they moved through the rooms, Dash kept up a running explanation of what they were seeing. At one point Ping whispered to Jam, "She knows more than the museum does. She's not learning anything, so why are we here again?"

Jam whispered back. "Because she enjoys teaching as much as she enjoys learning. We are her friends. Be her student for today. She needs it."

"Uh huh."

They came into the room with another large glassed-in model ship, the *GPlex I* herself. Built to same scale as the model of *The World*, she was visibly larger.

"There she is," Jam observed. "That's the ship we're on at this very moment."

Ping asked, "Where are we?" She peered inside. "Ah. There's a little arrow, see? 'You are here.' Cool!"

Dash had stepped away, intrigued by a large image of a group of people standing in front of the ship. At least, one could presume it was the ship, though only a small part of the superstructure loomed in the background of the tight photo. As Ping and Jam drifted over to her, Dash pointed. "The ribbon-cutting ceremony." She peered at the faces, matching them to the names in the caption. "Everyone involved in the autonomous mobile island movement–

known as *seasteading* at the time--was there." She started pointing. "Friedman. Quirk. Thiel."

Ping yawned. "Ancient history. They're all dead, right?"

As Dash looked into the center of the crowd, she saw a face that looked familiar. She gasped as she read the matching name, and pointed at the face.

Ping was looking around the room, bored, but Jam saw Dash's stabbing finger and leaned over to see.

The caption read, **Colin Wheeler, Project Director, BrainTrust**.

Jam looked at Dash. Dash looked at Jam. They both looked at Ping. Jam said dryly, "Yes, Ping, I'm sure you're right. Ancient history. I'm sure they're all dead."

Jam's cell phone beeped with a text message, which she studied briefly. "Ok, Dash, we have a recommendation for somewhere we should go next."

Ping whirled back to her friends in delight. "Awesome. Let's cruise!"

Jam followed the directions that had been texted to her phone. They took her onto the *FB Alpha*, up the elevator to the highest covered deck, then up a ramp onto the top deck, which Jam thought should just be called the roof.

Except that this deck should probably be called the "Hanging Gardens of Babylon." These gardens did not hang and were not in Babylon, but they were in their own way probably more remarkable than whatever Nebuchadnezzar II had built.

Perhaps it should be called the "Glory of the World

Garden" instead, because Jam was pretty sure there were flowers and shrubs from almost everywhere. Some sections had heaters to keep the vegetation in the temperature range of its homeland. Some had bright lights to enhance the sunlight to tropical levels. Other parts had misters to keep the flowers as well-watered as they needed to be. And some parts of the Garden had all three.

From the center of the garden you could see nothing else but sky if you looked up, and the lush spread of flowering plants seemed to go on forever.

Dash exclaimed in delight. "Bali! These are from my home." She pointed at a stand of plants that rose above their heads, with purple flowers edged in gray. "*Andong*. It has good medicinal properties." She turned and pointed at another thicket of shrubbery sporting densely packed branches covered in yellowish foliage which opened to star-shaped scarlet flowers. "*Soka*." She just stood there, breathing the familiar scents.

Jam looked around them, seeking the one structure that should stand high enough to be seen. "There's the dome." She pointed. "That's our destination."

Ping jumped up to look in the direction she had pointed. "A dome! Cool! Can we climb it?" She leaped again to see over the *andong*. "It looks like it would be fun to climb."

"Let's go find out," Jam encouraged. Ping ran ahead to check out possibilities.

"What's in the dome?" Dash asked.

"I am told it contains magic," Jam answered.

"I am skeptical."

"Of course."

They walked in companionable silence to their destination.

They saw a couple coming out, pushing hard on the door to open it and jumping out of the way as it swung closed. Clearly the door was meant to stay closed except for the briefest moments for entrance and exit.

Ping pulled on the door handle with both hands. "Allow me," she said as she dragged it open.

Passing inside, they found themselves inside a small alcove with another door at the far end; they stood in an airlock. Dash commented, "This is serious containment. How dangerous is the thing we are going to see, anyway?"

Jam pushed the inner door open. "All is now revealed."

Dash went through, crowded forward by Ping. The dome's walls and plants were covered with a dizzying array of colors, and more colors swirled through the air in an endless silent current that marched—or flew—to its own rhythm. It was so complex in aggregate that it was hard to pick out one patch to focus on.

Ping figured it out first. "Butterflies!"

Dash gasped, and even Jam stared in wonder. "Magic," Jam whispered.

Dash wore a smile as wide as an isle ship. "Magic. I accept your claim."

They walked slowly toward the center of the room, the current of colors whirling around them. Something about Dash's white lab coat seemed to attract the butterflies; one by one, they settled on her shoulders, her arms, and her head. "Monarch. Azure Hairstreak. Swallowtail. Birdwing." She named the orange and purple and yellow and green butterflies as they landed.

More butterflies settled upon her, and she instinctively spread her arms to give them more places to land. She turned her palms up, and half a dozen landed on her hands. As she turned to face her friends, her smile was so wide it hurt.

———

Amanda accompanied Colin to the botanical garden at the top of the *FB Alpha*. Amanda looked at him in amusement. "Time to stop and smell the roses?" she asked, not quite sarcastically.

"We don't do it often enough, do we?" Colin had a faraway look in his eyes. He bent to a pot of star jasmine and inhaled. "We forget many of the things we see, but very few of the things we scent."

"Colin?" Amanda tapped his arm to bring him back to the real world.

"You've heard about the results of her experiments?"

Amanda closed her eyes. "Yes." She sighed. "It's the price we pay for moving so fast. If we aren't careful, we'll turn as cautious as the dirtsiders in our horror at the cost to our patients. No more progress." She frowned at him. "But that's your lecture to give, not mine."

He did not answer, but moved purposefully toward the butterfly dome. "There they are," he murmured in satisfaction.

Amanda looked, but only saw the door swinging shut. "Who?"

Colin seemed unable to listen. "With the first four isle ships, even when we were cramming in people till they spilled out the gunwales, we filled the isle ships with places to play. 'Work hard, play hard' was our mantra. Water slides, climbing walls, dance floors—even an ice rink. But I knew we needed a place to play softly, too. A place to heal the soul." He opened the door for her.

Amanda nodded as she walked to the other end of the air lock. "Of course." She pushed open the inner door, then stopped dead as Colin joined her and she saw what was happening.

As they watched from afar, Dash stood utterly still while Jam and Ping and a handful of others took pictures of her clothed in butterflies. A young couple walked slowly around her, recording the scene for later 3D video creation.

Eventually Amanda whispered. "Did you plan this? All of this?"

He shook his head. "Just a nudge. I had no idea."

Amanda bumped shoulders with him mischievously. "So, is this why you wanted her here?"

"It was not." The slightly calculating look that rarely left his eyes softened, dimmed, and disappeared. "Until now."

8

CONFUSION UNTO OUR ENEMIES

If you can't join them, beat them.
—Helen Mound, *The Sunday Times*

The closest thing the Voice of the Silent had to a robotics expert was Jerry. Drew just hoped Jerry was up to the task.

Their plans to snag a hundred pounds of ammonium nitrate fertilizer had gone off the rails. They had underestimated the amount of supervision the movement and storage of fertilizer received. There was no way to snatch the stuff without being found out, not without at least two inside men. They had to change the plan. Grabbing the fertilizer would be their third-to-last operation, followed without pause by the making of the bombs and the assault on the hospital ship *Chiron*. They'd found the abortion clinic. It was on the Red Planet deck, adjacent to a hospital wing that had guards stationed around it as if there were things or people of great value there. Not that it made any difference to their plans; if they blew up something precious because it happened to be next to the clinic, so much the better. People would learn not to put anyone or anything they cared about too close to places of abomination in the future.

So Drew had rented a couple of bots, and Chuck had rented a half dozen arvans.

Now they would see if Jerry, God willing, could get what they needed.

Dash had been grinding through the autopsy data for more hours than she could count, trying to make sure they weren't missing anything from the deaths that might impact the lives of the remaining patients. Now it was the middle of the night. Dash sat at the conference table, wedged between Amanda and Byron. They were studying the results of Ryan's autopsy when Amanda's phone rang with an ominous tone. Amanda opened her phone and asked tensely, "What's wrong?" Amanda's phone was set to speaker, so Dash couldn't help listening in.

"Dr. Copeland, a few hours ago two bots dashed through the cargo dock while the day's shipment of fertilizer was being unloaded. They seemed half out of control, like a couple of teenagers were running them. As we have since reconstructed from the vidcams, the bots grabbed two canisters of ammonium nitrate and took off."

Amanda responded sharply. "Find the bots. Surely you can track them on the vidcams."

"Yes, ma'am, but they ran into an arvan lot that already had stacks of empty canisters. Those wouldn't normally have been present, so they must have been put there in advance. After a few minutes of hide and seek, half a dozen vans pulled out and headed in all directions. We're trying to track them all down, but we're behind the curve on this. We didn't realize the canisters had been stolen until after the arvans were long gone, so we're back-and-forward tracking on the vidcams now. Meanwhile, we're trying to track who rented the bots that did this. It'll take us at least an hour or two to figure out where the ammonium nitrate is and who took it."

Amanda stood up and started pacing. "Set Condition Yellow for the entire BrainTrust."

"Yes, ma'am." After a pause, the voice continued, "Done."

She stopped pacing at the far end of the room and dialed another number on her phone. "Colin, did you hear? We may have bombmakers on board." She listened. "Good idea. I'll close the docks and scatter the sniffer bots to look for the ammonium nitrate." Another pause. "Check. Diesel too. Yes, later." Amanda stabbed the End key. "I'm on my way to *Chiron's* Command Information Center." Amanda pursed her lips. "My rotation as Board Chairman started last week, so I seem to be in charge." She pointed at Dash. "Stay here. Colin is on his way."

Dash looked puzzled. "*Pak* Colin? Why?"

Amanda threw up her hands. "I have no idea." Then she was gone.

Colin trotted in with Ping and Jam in tow. Jam looked

as somber as Dash had ever seen her, but Ping looked so happy she seemed ready to bounce off the walls.

Dash looked at Colin. "Why are you here?"

Colin punched several buttons on his phone and slaved the screens on the walls to his unit. Amanda appeared on one of the screens and started speaking immediately. "It's worst case. A sniffer on *Elysian Fields'* promenade deck just detected both diesel and ammonium nitrate. It looks like they're heading to *Chiron.*" She took a deep breath, and said to someone off-screen, "Condition Red Defense of Ship protocol."

A klaxon sounded at an almost painful volume outside Dash's conference room. Ping said quietly but urgently, "I should get my guns."

Colin shook his head. "Stay with Dash. Unless I miss my guess, she's a target. Take her up to Blue Lagoon, the Omega conference room. I'll join you there momentarily."

Jam took command. "Let's go."

Dash pointed down the passage to the right. "The elevator's this way."

Jam pointed forcefully to Dash's left. "Use the ramp, girl. We don't want to get stuck on the elevator in Condition Red."

"We'd miss all the action," Ping explained.

Jam rolled her eyes but said nothing as they headed for the ramp.

Byron ran in the opposite direction, yelling to them over his shoulder. "I'll catch up with you in a few."

Ping, Jam, and Dash started running, then stopped as the walls of all the passages shimmered. One moment they were standing on Mars, harsh and unyielding, but the next moment the walls were covered with lush green jungle growth swaying in a light breeze. The image of a monkey stared down at them, and Dash clapped her hands. "Bali!"

Colin poked his head out of the conference room they'd just left. "Did it work?" He looked around. "I guess it did. We've been experimenting with full-wall-coverage digital paint for the deck themes, so we could switch them easily. Nice."

Dash looked at him sternly. "We are in Condition Red and people are running toward us with bombs, and you want to change deck themes?"

Colin smiled. "I told you a while ago I'd look into getting your research wing a Bali theme."

"Now there are two decks with the same theme right next to each other," Dash complained.

"No, I switched them. Deck Eleven is now Red Planet."

Dash still looked at him with exasperation, but Jam now looked at him with admiration. "Confusion to our enemies. *Allahu akbar!*"

"Hallelujah," Ping agreed.

The Emeryville Chapter of the ELC had gathered in Mary and Paul's quarters on the *Elysian Fields*. Paul patiently asked Peter the same question for the tenth time since they'd gotten here. "Are you sure you don't want to pop over to the *Argus* for a few minutes and use the 3D printers to roll off some guns?"

And for the tenth time, Mary turned apoplectic. Once again, she shouted the One True Answer before anyone else could get a word in. "Guns kill people! We can't be using guns!"

Peter shared a look with Paul, then glanced at the backpack bombs that were finally ready to go—the ones Mary was so excited to deliver. Peter muttered just for Paul, "Irony really *is* dead." Still, he did not argue in favor of Paul's plan because—and he acknowledged to himself that this too was ironic—he agreed with Mary.

A shrill klaxon split the air.

"What's that?" demanded Mary.

Justin answered, "Condition Red. The archipelago is under attack."

Peter decided immediately. "That's it, then. Grab your packs and let's go."

Paul looked doubtful. "With the guards running all over the place?"

Peter shrugged into his pack, his sense of urgency rising. "Either they're after us, in which case this is our last chance, or they're completely distracted going after somebody else, in which case this is our best chance. 'Confusion unto our enemies' and all that." He threw open the door. "Red Planet, here we come!" They all started to run, their poorly-tightened packs flopping against their backs.

Neither the running nor the flopping packs made them stand out. Tourists were already running in every conceivable direction, carrying ridiculous totes and packs.

Their SDV, the Seal Delivery Vehicle, did not surface. Lieutenant Rick Boehm and his fire team swam the last thirty feet to the dock of the *WarenHaus* isle ship.

Rick spit the regulator from his mouth and started cursing even before he removed his mask. He'd been cursing off and on ever since his fire team had gotten this assignment.

Talk about a royal clusterfuck! He'd heard stories of the tunnels of Tora Bora, trying to squeeze the terrorists out of that Afghanistan mountain complex in his father's day. That had been bad enough to keep anyone entertained, but this was going to be incredibly worse—or at least incredibly more ridiculous.

If each passageway on each of these isle ships was considered a tunnel, he was looking at five hundred miles of tunnels on the BrainTrust archipelago. He had to find one person in that welter of passages and kidnap her. Quietly. While minimizing civilian casualties. In a city with a hundred and twenty thousand people in its teeming masses.

And some of those people were children of senators belonging to the Red party. And Rick's team was running an assault on the medical center, where such children could easily wind up if they broke an arm or caught the flu. What could possibly go wrong?

At least these tunnels were not booby-trapped. Unless —he glanced overhead—you counted the vidcams everywhere. The vidcams couldn't kill you, but they could alert people who could.

Except—more good news—the security people didn't normally carry guns. On the downside, intel suggested that when they *did* carry guns, those guns were scary good, high-tech beyond anything in Seal Team Three's inventory. And in a few moments, when the vidcams carried images of his team to the Powers That Be, those security people would be trading out their batons for those beyond-state-of-the-art guns.

Perhaps even worse, the intel also suggested that the security people themselves were scary good, top caliber professionals from all over the world. Not that they could be as good as his own people, of course, but definitely not to be despised like some bunch of ragheads who thought shooting AK47s in the air at a birthday party constituted military training.

He led his team through the gangway into the *Waren-Haus*. As expected, this cargo-oriented ship did not have exotic deck themes like the ships with lots of people. The walls were simple gunmetal grey, even the wall behind the pudgy fellow in dungarees, who was sitting on a stool and working on a computer. *Damnation!*

Boehm stopped short. The pudgy fellow raised his eyebrows at him. "I don't think you're supposed to be here," he remarked companionably.

Four machine guns and a grenade launcher were leveled at the poor fellow. "Hands behind your back," Boehm commanded.

"As you wish." The pudgy worker stood slowly.

As Tommie zip-tied the fellow, he talked. Irritatingly. "You do realize that you're already on camera? You have maybe fifteen minutes before the peacekeepers are on you."

Rick already knew that, but he couldn't afford to show concern. It was part of his leadership training. He smiled wickedly. "I think we can handle some peacekeepers armed with batons."

The guy shook his head. "Haven't you ever heard of home court advantage?"

Time to hurry. "Bruce, vidcams," he commanded.

Bruce was already unlimbering his XCR assault rifle. *Bang, bang, bang,* and all the vidcams with a view of their current location were gone.

Two minutes later, all five members of the fire team were wearing the yellow shirts and black pants of the local cops over their armor. That might have been good news, except the equipment they were carrying was definitely not standard issue for the peacekeepers, so Boehm's people would still stand out like sore thumbs on the vidcams if anyone watching had a clue. But maybe no one would have a clue because—more good news—the intel team had kept the mission on hold until the moment they got word that a group of Green terrorists they'd been tracking were starting their assault on another part of the BrainTrust.

That was the only part of the plan he liked. The way the Greens spent their time soulfully spouting the wisdom of Mother Earth like a bunch of religious fanatics always pissed him off. How delightful it was that they were being useful for a change, if only as a distraction. Three cheers for confusion to everyone.

As they had hoped and expected, there wasn't anybody up and about at one in the morning on the cargo ship. The *WarenHaus* was the logistics ship, full of shipping containers. It had fewer residents than any ship other than *GPlex III* or *GSDC*, the two datacenter ships that were full of compute-servers. Those were almost entirely devoid of personnel.

Rick and his team had boarded the *WarenHaus* because it was the best combination of few bystanders, good docking, and proximity to the target.

They ran into the intersection between the port-to-starboard and fore-to-aft passageways. As they turned left, Rick glanced at his GPS and swore. As anticipated he had no signal, since they were running down a passage in the middle of a mountain of steel. Another quick check showed he had no coms either, not unless he wanted to interface with the BrainTrust's own cell or wifi systems, which everyone had agreed during planning would just be another way to fuck up.

Everyone on his team would have memorized all the maps of the archipelago's layout they could get their hands on anyway, but since they'd expected to lose signal, they'd paid extra-special attention while training on the mockup they'd built of the *WarenHaus* and the *Chiron* back in San Diego. At this moment they were not quite four hundred feet from the gangway that would take them onto the *Chiron*. If their intel was phenomenally good and they were phenomenally lucky, the target would be on the Red Planet deck on the *Chiron*. Get in, snatch the good doctor, get out while everyone was focused on the Green terrorists.

What were the chances that the intel would be that good? If the doc wasn't there, if she'd swapped shifts with another doc and gone off to party at Quark's, they were looking at a perfect FUBAR.

The fertilizer had arrived, and with careful haste, the Voice of the Silent completed their bombs. They congratulated each other as they strapped on their packs and donned their Stetsons in hopes that the hats would make vidcam recognition a little harder. Jerry said a few last words: "Psalms 18:48, folks. 'He delivers me from my enemies; Surely You lift me above those who rise up against me.'"

And then they were running through the decks.

In just a few minutes they were out of the *Elysian Fields* and onto the *Chiron's* Red Planet deck. No one seemed to have noticed them. Their attempt to confuse their enemies had apparently worked. Since they had left the *Elysian Fields*, the crowd density had rapidly thinned. Now that they were finally on the deck with the abortion clinic, there was no one around.

No one.

Chuck was the first to say it out loud. "Something's wrong."

Jerry slowed down but did not stop. "Trap?"

They turned the corner that should have brought them to the clinic, but all that faced them was a compartment with nothing but a few tables and chairs.

Drew answered. "Trap." He looked around. "How did they move all those people out of here?"

Charging feet came from two different directions, and several cops in their yellow shirts appeared from a side passage. Howie shouted, "Light 'em up!" After that, no one could hear anything above the din of gunfire.

The Emeryville Chapter of the ELC discovered the critical merit of physical fitness for operational elements of the Crusade on the way to the seared desert bleakness of the Red Planet deck. The good news was that they made it in only a handful of minutes. The bad news was that they were exhausted and gasping for breath. Peter felt like throwing up. He obviously sat on his butt too much as a software engineer; he needed to get more exercise.

The others were in about the same shape. Well, Mary and Paul were in about the same shape; Justin had fallen considerably behind. Peter glared at him, but Justin just stopped and bent over far down the corridor. Practically folded in half, Justin waved for him to continue. Peter rolled his eyes and trotted into the open area that would have the abortion clinic to the left and their target straight ahead.

It struck him that somehow this was the wrong deck. Or something had happened; there were no guards stationed where they'd been the last time, and the abortion clinic, which had bustled with people, was empty. The whole place was empty. Except for one little group.

A bunch of cowboys had tramped in moments before them, and now stopped dead. They carried shiny guns and dull gray backpacks not unlike his own. The cowboys stared into the empty clinic, apparently as confused as he was.

Then a bunch of cops came out of a passage on the far side, bristling with weapons like no other cops he had ever seen anywhere. *Christ!*

Paul asked, "Trap?" He seemed doubtful.

Peter shook his head. "Weirder than that."

The cowboys started shooting at the cops, the cops started firing back, and Peter threw himself desperately to the floor.

All the screens in the Omega conference room were lit up. Ping and Jam hovered near the door. Dash sat in a chair at the table, leaning forward as if to take action, then rocking back again as she realized there was nothing she could do. Byron, having caught up with them as promised, had slid around the conference table to the far side, where he alternated sitting and pacing. Colin stood staring at the screen showing the open area in Deck Eleven, which was now the Red Planet deck. Amanda yelled from another screen. "Colin, is this your doing?"

Colin shrugged. "Well, I suppose it would be inappropriate to make a joke about it right now." He paused. "None of our people are in danger, and at least we have good seats." They watched as the group dressed like Red-state cowboys opened fire.

"Sweet Jesus!" Lieutenant Boehm shouted as he skidded halfway to a stop. Then, seeing the nutcases in cowboy hats and jeans level their weapons, he shifted direction from a left turn into a straight sprint to duck into the side passage across from where they'd entered.

The sounds of gunfire and ricochets filled the area. He

knelt by the corner and stuck his rifle into the main passage so his scope could pick up a view of the scene.

Bruce had crossed the main passage slightly behind Rick, but not quite in time to avoid getting nicked by a spent bullet. He limped over to Rick.

Shaun was lying in the open, blood pouring from his chest. When the firing stopped for a moment Tommie crawled partway out to him, grabbed his leg, and dragged him back. Casey then knelt by the corner in the passage they'd come out of hefting his Xm25G grenade launcher.

The cowboy nutcases were quickly building a barricade of tables and chairs.

As Rick swiveled his rifle, he saw, coming from yet another passage, a gaggle of twenty-something geeks wearing t-shirts, shorts, and Birkenstocks. They looked clueless, though at least one of them had thrown himself to the deck when the cowboys opened up. *Oh, shit.* One of the geeks sagged to the floor as if she'd been hit. *Dammit, this was what he'd been afraid of.* Innocent bystanders.

The mission was blown, and he didn't even understand how it had happened. Who were those lunatics with the titanium rifles? They had to be titanium, from the glimpse he'd gotten; that silver-gray sheen was reasonably distinctive.

But it didn't make any difference who they were; they had to be stopped. For all he knew, that kid who'd just taken a bullet was one of the senators' kids. Not his mission, but well within his purview given the circumstances.

The original mission plan had included a contingency if the doctor wasn't on this deck. If possible, they were to make their way to the Appalachian Springs deck to see if the doctor was at home, then get the hell out, with or without her. But first he had to deal with these trigger-happy yahoos shooting at anything that moved and killing bystanders.

"Casey," he hissed. "Take out those idiots behind the barricade."

Casey stuck his head and his launcher into the passage. The nutjobs opened fire again, but Casey got his shot off. He had not quite withdrawn back into the corridor when the grenade reached its optimal detonation point.

The Xm25G grenade launcher was not so much a smart gun as a clever one. It was designed to hit targets safely ensconced behind bulletproof barriers: the rifle computed the distance to the barrier, estimated its thickness, and programmed the grenade to explode after passing over the barrier into the safe space where the enemy lay in complacent confidence.

About ten percent of the time something went wrong. This was not one of those times; it worked perfectly. As a consequence, the Voice of the Silent ceased to exist moments later.

Unfortunately, this perfect operation also meant that one of the fertilizer bombs, hit by the compression wave in just the right way, triggered. The resulting explosion was considerably larger than would be expected from the detonation of a mere grenade. Indeed, the explosion was large enough to involve the other three fertilizer bombs, creating a composite explosion astonishingly larger than might be expected. Large enough, as it happened, to trigger the peroxide bombs carried by Peter, Paul, and Mary.

"Inferno" was an inadequate description of the resulting chain reaction.

The Blue Lagoon deck shook momentarily. No one in the Omega conference room quite lost their footing, though Byron muttered, "Earthquake."

Most of the vidcams on the entirety of Deck Eleven ceased transmitting as a blink of brilliant whiteness swept the open area. Perversely, one camera close to the barricade flickered and maintained its focus on the charcoal remains of the people who had once hidden there. Ping was the first to understand what the camera was showing. "Whoa!" she exclaimed. "Burnt bacon bits."

Jam shook her head. "What are bacon bits?"

Ping pursed her lips. "Take some dulse, chop it up into small pieces, and fry the pieces until till they're burnt." It was the best analogy for someone who'd never had bacon.

Dash scrutinized the scene. "Yes, burnt dulse bits makes an adequate depiction." Her expression was one of clinical dismay.

The little vidcam that had survived so much flickered into darkness.

Lt. Rick Boehm still did not understand how they'd missed

the turn to the *WarenHaus* dock. They'd still been dazed when they came to the simple right turn that would carry them to their SDV and safety. As nearly as Rick could figure, they'd turned left instead.

By the time his head had fully cleared, they were into the *GPlex III*. They could hear voices behind them shouting commands. "I think going back is contraindicated," he muttered in an attempt at lightheartedness.

It was a pretty weak attempt. After the explosion—or rather, after the explosions, which just seemed to go on and on like an artillery barrage—he'd known the mission was blown. If his target had been anywhere near where she was supposed to be, she was now dead. But he suspected that was not the correct interpretation.

His men's body armor had more or less saved them. Once Rick's head had cleared just enough to be able to distinguish blood from water, he'd crawled to their bodies. Shaun had been bleeding out. Rick had shot the wounds he could find with FoamClot, but he had no idea whether that had been enough or not. Half of Casey's face was burnt black; it was lucky that he was unconscious. Horrified, Rick had sprayed his face with InstaSkin. It was all he could do.

By the time he'd finished with Casey, Bruce had Tommie up and staggering back the way they'd come. Bruce was helping Tommie, but Bruce was badly hurt himself; a FoamClot patch on his left leg testified to that.

Tommie was not bleeding, but the blasts had knocked his helmet off. Rick himself was dazed, but Tommie was in much worse shape, swaying as he tried to stand. Rick took Tommie's left arm, Bruce took his right, and the three of them hobbled out of there back toward the *WarenHaus*.

But now they were aboard the *GPlex III*—of that at least, Rick was sure. The *GPlex III* was a pure compute-server ship, and quite distinct from the ships designed for residents. The promenade was not broad or packed with shops and people. Rather, the gray-walled promenade was just wide enough for a pair of the ubiquitous arvees to pass each other. There were supposedly people deep in the bowels of the ship maintaining the servers, but they only came through here as they went to and from their cabins. At the moment, the passages were empty.

Boehm's briefing had included little information on the *GPlex III* and the other server ship, the *GSDC*. Intel had been unable to procure any information about the internal layouts of the server ships beyond minimal info about the public passages. The public passages and the promenade interconnected in the standard fashion with the other ships so people could pass through, but all the doors to the server systems were sealed. No one but the maintenance people got through those doors.

Intel wasn't even sure if there were vidcams in the promenade, having acquired conflicting reports. Looking around, Boehm could not see any, but that did not constitute proof they weren't there. This ship held vital GPlex secrets; it seemed unlikely that GPlex was blind to events here.

Rick closed his eyes and visualized the map of the BrainTrust again. Behind him was the *WarenHaus* with people chasing him; not a good path to take. To the right was the *GPlex II*, packed with people; another bad choice.

The left was tempting. There was an artificial beach in the space where another isle ship could have docked. Reach the beach, turn right, scamper across it and dive into the patch of open ocean that occupied another isle-ship-sized hole in the BrainTrust archipelago. The beach would be empty. During the day the beach would be packed with swimmers and sunbathers, but no one would be there in the dead of night except perhaps a few adventurous lovers. It was very tempting indeed.

But there was no cover. Snipers on any of the three isle ships in proximity would have absurdly easy shots while they crossed the beach to the ocean patch. The risk of being spotted in the open was the reason they'd rejected it as an entry point in the first place and come in through the *WarenHaus*.

If they could get to the open ocean, they were home free. The DSV would hear them hit the water. They could dive, and in minutes they could be out of there. But not across the beach.

Straight ahead was the gangway to the *GSDC*. Turning left in the *GSDC* would take them straight into the beach-side ocean without risking exposure on the beach itself.

As he explored his options, Tommie's eyes rolled back in his head, which lolled forward. Boehm and Bruce let him down gently on the deck. Rick spoke to himself as much as to Bruce. "He'll be all right. The BrainTrusters are not murderers. They'll take care of him."

"Really?" Bruce sounded dubious.

"It's not like we have a choice anymore. Let's get out of here and report." He pointed forward. Bruce limped along beside him and they soon entered the *GSDC* as they listened to voices approach from behind.

Colin swore as he watched the three Seals turn left into the *GPlex III* rather than turning right to get back to the dock they'd started from. Peacekeepers were ready and waiting on the dock. Whoever was in charge of the Seals must have deduced somehow that their entry point was now a trap. "Amanda," he said more loudly than made sense, given that she was just a microphone away. "They're heading into *GPlex III*. We need eyes."

"We certainly do." On the screen, Amanda glanced at someone to her right. "I hereby authorize, for the duration of this Condition Red Defense of Ship, integration of the vidcams from *GPlex III* and *GSDC*."

A voice off-screen argued, "They aren't going to like that, Doctor Copeland."

She shrugged. "It's part of their contract. They can complain after we're done if they're overly excited about it."

The screens in Omega switched views to *GPlex III*. The Seals were making remarkably good time, considering how beat up they were.

What else could go wrong?

Another voice spoke from off-screen. "Dr. Copeland, we think someone actually survived from Group Two and got away. He's wearing a backpack like the others in Group Two. We hypothesize it's a peroxide bomb."

Ask a silly question.

Justin had been gasping for breath forever. The stitch in his side was now so painful he could hardly take a step. He half-fell off the ramp onto the deck and saw no down-ramp. Perhaps this was indeed the bottom of the ship.

The walls were icy white with occasional slashes and bubbles of pale blue-green peeking through the crystal faces; a Tundra-themed deck. Beautiful in its own coldly austere way, it was yet another of the Earth's infinitely varied forms of beauty.

Justin had come to realize—even before the disaster on the Red Planet deck—that whoever had told Peter the nukes were up there had been telling him a whopper. That was one of the reasons he'd used to justify to himself slowing down and falling behind his friends in their race plant their bombs. When his friends disappeared in a blazing inferno, he knew what he would do. As he'd told them, the nukes had to be in the pylons jutting out the bottom of the ship. He would go down there, find one, and finish the job.

He touched his nose gingerly. The blazing explosion had almost finished him as well as everyone else, burning his face to the point where his lips and nose were cracked and raw. His eyebrows were gone. He was just glad he couldn't see himself in a mirror.

He couldn't just run around on the Tundra deck hoping to find the hatch to one of the nukes. He tried to visualize where he was in relation to the bow and match that against the location of the forward pylon, one-third of the distance to the stern. Logical analysis led him swiftly to an unerring conclusion.

He was lost.

He started jogging toward what he thought was the bow, though he confessed to himself it was just as likely he was jogging toward the stern. That would be okay. If he were amidships, the pylons would be equidistant in both directions, and he didn't care which one he found as long as there was a nuke plant inside.

Justin generally believed that luck favored the prepared, but today luck had seemed to favor him despite his lack of preparation. He quickly stumbled upon a hatch surrounded by warning signs, some of them displaying the traditional yellow-and-black radiation alert.

Of course the damn hatch was dogged tight and padlocked, but this did not bother him as much as it might have. He had foreseen the possibility that there would be a locked door or two between his friends and their destination. His hydrogen peroxide bombs were not ideal for blowing locks, but they would suffice, particularly when used in combination with a coil of magnesium ribbon he had brought for just that purpose. Magnesium burned with a brilliant white 3100-degree flame; he would use his tiniest bomb to set off the magnesium, which would melt the padlock's shackle.

A couple minutes later, standing at a distance from the flare, he could see through his closed eyelids that the burn was finished. He opened his eyes to good news. Gingerly kicking the remains of the lock away, he undogged the hatch.

At that point, though, his luck began to run out.

Someone shouted at him from down the passage, so it was definitely time to finish. He could see plumbing and machinery; the pylon was not just a giant lump of concrete to keep the ship stable in high seas. It was a nuke. He set the timer on the main bomb in his backpack, tossed it into the well of the pylon, and slammed the hatch shut.

Cops ran up, pounded him mercilessly to the ground, flipped him, and cuffed him. They were struggling to drag him back to his feet when a muffled *Boom* came from below and the deck shuddered. Everyone fell, and Justin laughed somewhat maniacally. The ruptured nuclear core was releasing radioactive waste as they stood here. He and the cops would be the first to die, but it was okay. The Earth had been saved.

The molten salt nuclear reactor sat in the thick-walled, confined space at the core of the pylon. As Justin had expected, it was a perfect environment for a hydrogen peroxide bomb. The explosion wreaked terrible havoc on the upper half of the power plant. The upper half was full of power-generation machinery, separated from the nuclear core itself by a thick slab of concrete. And while the bomb did not blast the core and its lower-deck support structure with anything approaching the force it unleashed on the upper area, the explosion *did* breach the concrete divider. The core shook.

But there was no secondary explosion. Since the reactor operated at normal atmospheric pressure, there was no containment vessel that would burst when ruptured and spread contaminants for miles. Rather, the viscous lithium fluoride salt merely quivered in its comparatively thin vessel, a container designed specifically to keep the liquid in a semi-spherical shape. That spherical shape was necessary to keep the neutron capture rate high enough to sustain the chain reaction.

Several additional things happened more or less at once. The supercritical CO_2 turbine that generated the power splintered into a thousand pieces. Without power, not only did the lights go out, but the cooling system that kept the freeze plug in the base of the reactor vessel from melting failed and the plug started to go.

The CO_2 that drove the turbine escaped, not quite explosively since it primarily departed through the remains of the turbine. As it rushed out, it created a sound that, had anyone been there to listen, would have been described as a very loud hissing.

The CO_2 acted as the coolant for the molten core, so when the coolant departed, the core's temperature rose rapidly. In the old movies about obsolete styles of nuclear reactors this would have led to a meltdown of the core, but here the core was already molten, so nothing so dramatic ensued. Rather, the rapidly heating liquid of the core expanded, as liquids do when the temperature rises. As the liquid expanded, more neutrons escaped without initiating fission, breaking the chain reaction. The core then cooled as rapidly as it had heated moments earlier, following a mathematically inescapable consequence of the physics and the chemistry of the reactor.

The spherical vessel holding the liquid core was, as noted earlier, relatively thin. The explosion that utterly savaged the upper deck mildly torqued it. The torque was enough to cause several cracks to form, and hot core fluid started to leak through. As it dripped out, since it was no longer part of the carefully shaped core, all the neutrons it generated were lost, further reducing the ability of the core to sustain a nuclear reaction.

The plug at the bottom of the vessel, which had started melting earlier, now dissolved completely away and the core started flowing out of the vessel. The flowing liquid joined the drips from the cracks as they fell onto a bed of boron sand, which absorbed the neutrons like a hungry frog catching mosquitoes. All nuclear chain reactions ceased, and the reactor started cooling irrevocably.

The vibrations from the explosion had damaged the sensors that watched for catastrophic failures. The clamps that held the pylon to the ship blew away, and the pylon sank rapidly into the darkening depths of the sea. Several small plugged holes popped open under the increasing pressure of the depth. Water flowed in, eliminating any pressure differential between the exterior and the interior of the pylon. Consequently, the pylon was not crushed by the water pressure as the depth increased.

The pylon continued to sink till it hit the ocean floor, where it caused an enormous splash of slow-moving mud. Inside, the lithium fluoride cooled enough to start to solidify. The pylon settled into a quiet state of equilibrium.

The radiation level around the pylon rose slightly. The sparse plant life at the bottom of the dark sea bloomed just a little in the enhanced radiation. In the next five years, a mutated form of diatom evolved, which thrived in the radiation. It flourished as long as it did not drift too far from the warm radiation of the pylon. The diatoms that drifted too far died and sank to the bottom of the sea.

The passages of the *GSDC* were as silent and gray and empty as the ones in the *GPlex III* and the *Warenhaus*, but Lieutenant Boehm really disliked one change in the layout of this ship. For whatever reason, the passages and the promenade they were entering were two decks high. The catwalk around the edge of the second deck would give a team of ambushers a magnificent field of fire.

The voices behind them sounded more distant. Bruce stumbled, then sagged. "I need a moment," he said.

Boehm led him into the shallow alcove next to one of the locked doors.

Bruce cursed. "Lieutenant, look at the door."

Boehm looked at the door. Very solid, like the doors they'd seen on the *GPlex III*, and indeed just like the doors on every ship they'd passed through. Except...he put his hand out to touch it. It was not as cold as the other doors, as if it weren't made of cold steel, but rather something warmer. Not plastic, but pottery, a ceramic of some type. Now it was the lieutenant's turn to curse. "Chobham armor? Are you kidding me?"

"No, sir. These doors—and the walls too, I think—are armored like our heaviest battle tanks. If we'd needed to breach the door for some reason, our whole team wouldn't have had enough explosives to get through." Bruce paused. "Why would they do this? It'd be ungodly expensive. They didn't even do this on the GPlex server ship, and that ship contained billions of dollars' worth of GPlex secrets."

Boehm pursed his lips. "It's the money."

"Sir?"

"The *GSDC* is packed with financial servers. This is one of the most important financial centers in the world. It's almost the only place where unfettered deregulated exchanges can still take place." Boehm took a breath. "There are trillions of dollars' worth of transactions going through here, Sergeant. *Trillions*. The *GPlex III* we just ran through is a mom-and-pop operation compared to this."

Bruce closed his eyes. "What are the chances, sir, that this empty place that's worth trillions only has strong passive defenses? Wouldn't they put in more, ah, aggressive countermeasures as well?"

Boehm pulled Bruce's arm across his own shoulders and moved out. "Time to go. Go go *go!*"

They entered the promenade and turned left. They were so close to the water; if they could just make it to the gangway that opened on the empty ocean! They ran. In moments they could see the open gangway. Boehm could even see a high-dive platform some lunatic had put there.

But it was not meant to be. Boehm was not surprised when, for the second time that night, a deafening staccato of gunfire sounded from just about everywhere. Bullets flew, ricocheting back and forth off the bulkheads, sizzling all around them. As they crouched, Boehm saw a neat circle of spent bullets, massively deformed from their complex flight around the deck, lying around them.

Oh, dear God. The intel guys had briefed them on rumors that the BrainTrust had developed a new generation of rifles just for shipboard action. The new rifles had scopes integrated with the ship's vidcams. They analyzed the area in 3D and computed all the ricochets, all the places and things the bullets would strike, and where they would land. Boehm, like every sensible person in the briefing, had discounted the idea. Those calculations were just too difficult; the data had to be too precise. It simply wasn't possible—but here was the proof. A neat circle of lead, with nary a one striking the two people in the middle of the circle.

He looked up to try to spot the shooters, but of course the shooters didn't have to stick their heads up to aim. They could just bounce the bullets, based on the ship's vidcams, off the ceiling. Boehm had no targets.

Then a head popped up on the overhead catwalk. The man revealed himself, standing tall. He carried a clunky-looking weapon and wore a charcoal gray pinstripe suit with a rich yellow power tie. "The Goldman Sachs Gun Club welcomes you, and offers you the chance to surrender." His face beamed. "Yippee-ki-yay, motherfucker."

Rick Boehm was about to be killed or captured by a goddam financial tycoon wearing a three-piece suit and spouting quotes from his father's favorite movie. This would become the new definition of "clusterfuck." He put down his rifle and clasped his hands behind his head. Then he picked up where he had left off on the dock, cursing this assignment.

Dash, along with everyone else in the Omega conference

room, watched as the Goldman Sachs Gun Club took the Seals prisoner. Colin remarked, "Not what I would have expected, but certainly within acceptable parameters. Amanda, as soon as they have the Seals off the *GSDC*, you can probably terminate the Condition Red."

Amanda looked apoplectic. "Thank you for stating the obvious." She looked around her CIC, then turned back to Colin with rage in her eyes. "We're done here. Get out of my sight." All the Omega screens driven by CIC feeds went blank.

Colin turned to the others. "That's a wrap," he said cheerfully. "Please return to your previously scheduled programming."

Dash stood up. "That was…interesting. Can we avoid this kind of excitement in the future?"

Colin held his hands out placatingly. "I do apologize, but I am hopeful that as we spread the word of what happened here tonight to the various parties that should have helped prevent this, they'll be embarrassed enough to do better in the future."

Jam looked at Colin thoughtfully. "Who were all those people?"

"I think we'll find, when the dust settles, that one group were Green eco-terrorists intent on turning the BrainTrust into a radioactive wasteland, and the other was a Red anti-abortion group planning to destroy the clinic next to your lab."

Dash said, "That is all good. It is hard to feel much sympathy for the people who were turned into, uh, burnt dulse bits. But what about the others? The ones dressed as peacekeepers?"

Colin's eyes clouded over. He spoke softly. "Dash, they were here for you."

Dash's eyes widened. "For me?"

"The Chief Advisor planned to kidnap you to rejuvenate the President-for-Life. It was their only chance to continue to hold power."

Dash looked at him in disbelief. "That is crazy!"

Jam commented, "That does not make him wrong."

Byron spoke in a voice harder than any she had ever heard from him. "It's not crazy at all. We've talked about this, Dash. Your rejuvenation therapy is the most terrible weapon ever unleashed on humankind. The President-for-Life can stay president forever, and the Chief Advisor can rule without end. The Blues will never be able to gain control and fix our country. We'll never be free if you complete your research." His eyes glittered with tears he refused to shed. "Which is why—" He pulled a gun from behind his back and started to fire.

Bang. Dash staggered back from a bullet to her abdomen. Colin leaped in front of her.

Bang. A bullet caught Colin in the chest. Jam ran to him.

Bang bang. As Jam pushed Colin and Dash to the ground, two bullets hit her in the back. Ping flipped over the conference table and spun in front of Byron. The baton in her right hand slammed into his gun and sent it flying, and the knife in her left sliced backward across his neck to send blood spurting all over the table. She completed her spin by bouncing her back and her head against the far wall as Byron fell to the deck.

Dash was lying on her back, half-buried under Colin and Jam. She looked under the table at Byron's fallen body.

Grievously wounded she might be, but she still had a surgeon's eye and made a surgeon's assessment. "I can save him," she croaked.

Ping shook her head to clear it and jumped forward to plunge the knife into Byron's heart. Blood gushed out to cover half her face.

Dash glared at Ping, then her eyes rolled up and she passed out.

9

HARMONY IN BALANCE

Problems cannot be solved at the same level of awareness that created them.
  —Albert Einstein

Sitting in his tiny cell in the tiny brig, Jamal had felt and heard the vibrations of a powerful explosion. It had been followed by a series of smaller vibrations, like a string of firecrackers. Then, somewhat later, there had been another *boom* and more shaking.

He'd had no idea how dangerous living on the Brain-Trust could be. His brother had been beaten and scarred by a prostitute, his best friend had been mutilated by a young girl, and now the whole ship was under attack. Multiple attacks.

His dark mood lightened. Given all the violence, it seemed a real possibility that his ex-wife would get killed in the fighting. Or, as an alternative, he as an innocent bystander would get killed as collateral damage of one battle or another.

That would not be a bad outcome. He might still get into Heaven, and he would not have to explain what had happened when he got home.

Joshua sat behind his desk wondering if perhaps he could arrange to swap ship jurisdictions with another mediator for a few months. Surely the wealth of too-interesting cases he was experiencing should be shared. Perhaps Mediator Chibuzo would be interested.

He cleared his throat. "The days may change, but the members of the cast remain the same." He started from left to right. "Amanda. Ms. Jam. Ms. Jam, we are so well acquainted I shall take you up on your earlier offer to just call you Jam."

Jam looked a little too stiff to him. "Jam, are you all right?"

Her whole body tensed as she answered very slowly. "Yes, sir. Just…a few…bruises, sir."

Amanda glared at her. "And two fractured ribs, let's not forget. She took two bullets, fortunately stopped by her vest. Still, she belongs in bed in her cabin."

"As soon as…the mediator…no longer needs…me."

Joshua spoke softly. "I've read your report, Jam. Well written, by the way. I think we can dispense with your presence."

Jam shook her head slightly. "Defend…Ping."

Joshua rolled his eyes. "All right. Let us move along." He looked to the right. "Justin Reed. Lieutenant Boehm. And of course, Ping." Of course, always Ping. He turned to Amanda. "There have been a shocking number of deaths this time, Amanda. Doesn't Colin want to be here for this one?"

Amanda stiffly answered, "He's in the hospital. Just coming off a ventilator. A bad bullet wound. He's lucky to be alive."

"Oh. I'm very sorry. Please give him my condolences." Seeing the rage in her eyes, he amended this. "Or at least as much condolence as you deem appropriate, given your estimate of how much he had to do with this situation."

Amanda snorted.

Joshua turned his attention to Justin, whose face was burnt, cracked, and puffy. "Mr. Reed. If this were an American court you would be charged with terrorism with a weapon of mass destruction. Amusing, is it not, that when you sabotage a nuclear reactor with a backpack bomb, American jurisprudence claims the backpack bomb is a WMD? But I digress. As a mediator, I am not empowered to assess such a case, so you are merely charged with sabotage of a ship of the BrainTrust." He frowned. "Ideally I would charge you the cost of the damage, but the damage is so immense you could not cover even a tiny fraction of it."

Justin eyed him, then asked, "How many people have died? How many more will die in the future?" He licked his severely chapped lips. "How big is the zone of radiation poisoning?" He licked his lips again, apparently to no effect. "I know we're in the middle of a hot zone, because I felt the ship start to move away earlier. You're trying to escape, aren't you? Is the reef dying?" He smiled happily.

Joshua wondered if Justin might get off on an insanity plea when he went dirtside. "You are hereby remanded to the custody of the FBI in the United States." Joshua looked over at Amanda. "I know you were unhappy about sending Jam's husband back to Pakistan, but this is quite different. The Reds would just execute him. The Blues would lock him up forever. Even the Greens would put him away for half his life."

Amanda shrugged. "I think that will be fine, Joshua."

"Take him away." After Justin was gone, Joshua decided to ask Amanda a question that he supposed was inappropriate to the proceedings. The answer would probably be healthy for the mental states of everyone in the room, however. "Is there any truth in what Justin just said? I felt us start to move too. Are we in the middle of a radiation cloud?"

"No, not at all. The failsafes worked as expected." She hesitated. "They worked so well, in fact, that they've become part of our rollout marketing campaign for the mass production and sale of small cheap safe nuclear reactors around the globe. Think about it. Our molten salt reactor didn't just shut down safely during a terrorist attack, it shut down safely after the terrorist had *achieved complete success* in sabotaging it. It's like Rhett has been saying for years: they're not only safer than coal plants and methane storage tanks, they're safer than solar cell production." She sighed. "Dash has been explaining that to me as well."

Joshua had another question, but was painfully aware

of Lieutenant Boehm's watchful presence. He waved Amanda over for a short sidebar, and peered at her suspiciously. "So everything worked out fine. Why aren't you happy about it?" he whispered.

Amanda let her gaze drift away. "The safety story with the sabotage is so compelling, it's made our rollout a huge success. We already have enough advance orders booked to pay for replacing the lost reactor." She whispered wonderingly, "Did Colin plan it? Even the loss of the reactor?"

Joshua stared at her. "Are you going to ask him?"

She shook her head. "If he did, I don't want to know." She closed her eyes. "Surely he did not. How could he? No, it's not possible." She opened her eyes. "It's not."

Joshua was glad that was unambiguously cleared up. "So if we actually tried to get damages from Justin, his advocate could reasonably argue that there were no damages since he supplied such excellent advertising that the injured parties have already received more than ample compensation. It would be an interesting case. I'm glad to dispense with it." He waved her back and addressed the room once more. "Let us move on and consider the fate of Lieutenant Boehm. Lieutenant?"

Lieutenant Boehm stood stiffly. "Yes, sir."

"First, let me tell you that all your people are still alive and recovering from their wounds as well as one could hope. I'll let you see them when these proceedings are over." After giving the lieutenant a moment to process this good news, Joshua continued. "Since you invaded the BrainTrust without signing a mediation agreement, I technically have no standing to mediate or render a verdict. But I can make a recommendation to the Board. You're guilty of state-sponsored piracy on the high seas. The Board may decide, for sufficient benefits, to send you home. Or to make a point, they may send you to the World Court, or any of the many countries I'd expect would be happy to try you on these charges."

Amanda interjected, "Indeed, a number of them have already shown up to offer support." She used her phone to control the main side screen and brought up the view to the southeast of the BrainTrust. The American cruiser that had been stationed there for several months, shadowed by a pair of tiny California Coastal Patrol ships, now had beefier company. A Russian cruiser paced the American. The two California ships each had a Chinese frigate as a friendly companion sharing their patrol duties. "As you can see, the balance of firepower has tipped for the moment. The French are even sending their aircraft carrier for a visit. And the Brits." Amanda paused, relishing her next words. "A British submarine surfaced and docked with the *Chiron* for an afternoon. They sent the Board its compliments, gave a few tours, and submerged again."

"Do you think they'll hang around?"

Amanda shrugged. "Who knows? If you were the Chief Advisor, what would you guess?"

Joshua laughed. "Very nice." He looked at Boehm. "Lieutenant, you are remanded into the custody of the Brain-Trust until the Board decides what to do. Guards, please take him to see his people, then return him to the brig."

After the Lieutenant had departed, he turned to the next case. "Ms. Ping," he said sternly.

Ping came to attention, more or less. "Yes, sir!" she chirped.

"You killed a resident."

"Yes, sir! Defense of Ship, sir!"

"With an unauthorized lethal weapon."

Ping looked a little sheepish. "It was an accident."

Joshua looked very stern. "An accident? Nothing about your assault on Byron Schultz was accidental."

"No, sir. I killed him quite intentionally, but it was an accident that I was carrying the knife. I was taking it to show Dash the cool folding on the blade."

"Dash? The surgeon who was in here a few days ago?"

"Yes, sir. The knife I used in the Defense of Ship action was the one you gave us, sir."

Joshua just stared at her. "The *chura* taken for compensatory damages from Jam's husband?"

Jam interrupted, "Ex-husband."

"Ex-husband," Joshua echoed, hopefully without the tinge of exasperation he felt.

Ping answered, "Yes, sir, the *chura*."

After pondering the matter for a few moments, Joshua decided to let it go. "Still, after incapacitating the resident, multiple eyewitness accounts say Dr. Dash told you she could save him, even after what would have appeared to the untrained eye to be a fatal injury." He was depending on witnesses because the conference room in which the battle had taken place was private, not public, and there had been no BrainTrust vidcams in operation at the time. "It sounds like you went out of your way to kill a helpless man."

Ping bowed her head submissively. Joshua wondered if she had ever done that before. It seemed unlikely. She answered, "I did not hear her—or to be more exact, I was not listening. I heard Dash say something, but I'm still not sure what she said except for what Jam has since told me. I was busy." She looked at Joshua. "I was…overwhelmed… with the need to guarantee that Byron could not continue his attack. I didn't know whether he was dead or if he could be saved, or anything. I just knew I needed to make sure he couldn't hurt anyone anymore." She paused, opened her mouth to say more, closed it, then opened her mouth again as a look of pain crossed her face. "I apologize."

Joshua sat back in wonder. "'And the waters parted, and they walked across the dry land.' We live in an age of miracles. Ms. Ping has apologized." He considered. "My contract with the BrainTrust gives me wide latitude to punish and command crew members. It's much more extensive than what I can do with residents and guests." He twitched his nose contemplatively. "You are required to take two weeks of administrative leave. Take some time to consider what you might have done differently. I leave it to your superiors to decide whether your leave should be paid or unpaid." He knocked his block of wood on the table. "These proceedings are over."

Dash could feel herself breathing. She thought that was good, if a little surprising. She tried to open her eyes, and failed. Focusing her will, she tried to open her eyes again, and this time she succeeded. A double-blurred image of a tall blond woman appeared in her vision. If someone held up their hand and asked Dash how many fingers they were holding up, Dash would kick them with all four feet.

The tall blond woman spoke in a whisper. "It was his own gun, as it turns out. He had it in the armory. When the Condition Red went off, he retrieved it and brought it to the conference room."

Dash recognized the voice. "*Bu* Amanda," she tried to whisper, but no sound came out.

Jam's voice whispered back, upset. "And I was too busy worrying about the invaders to worry about possible traitors, so I didn't notice it." The voice came from Dash's right. With another major effort, she rolled her head to see.

Jam and Amanda both spotted the movement. "Dash!" they both cried as loudly as they could while still whispering.

Dash's double vision retracted into proper focus as Amanda's face turned stern. "You're awake. About time. It's not like you were hit with a howitzer, just a simple through-and-through on the right side." She reconsidered. "Though you're such a tiny thing, for you it was a little like getting hit by a three-pounder naval cannon."

Dash tried to clear her throat. Jam moved stiffly over, grabbed a water glass with a straw, and offered it to her. After taking a couple sips, Dash asked, "Byron?"

Amanda shook her head. "By the time Ping got done, all the king's horses and all the king's men—" She stopped, probably realizing the reference was too exotic for present company. "Byron was already dead. Sometimes, of course, we can still save them even after they're dead. Not this time."

Dash heard some scuffling, then Ping's pixie grin bent over her. "Don't expect me to apologize."

A feminine arm with a bracelet of bangles pulled Ping out of the way, and Jam spoke. "Nor *should* she apologize, though a little bit less glee might be in order."

Dash rolled her eyes to see Jam. "Two shots," she muttered as she dug through her memories from just before she had passed out in Omega. "You took two shots. How can you…"

Jam spun, ever so carefully, in place. "Bulletproof vest, of course. Put it on when we went to Condition Yellow, since I'm a peacekeeper."

Amanda interjected, "A peacekeeper who is currently disobeying orders." She looked at Dash. "She ought to be in the bed next to yours."

Dash took a deeper breath. "*Pak* Colin?"

A choked, muffled laugh came from the other side of the curtain separating Dash from the next patient.

Amanda growled. "I figured you'd be asking about him when you woke up, so I broke a few rules—I can do that you know, I'm the boss and you should remember that—so here he is." She threw back the curtain. "You're awake now too, I take it."

Colin lifted a limp hand and tugged his oxygen mask down. "Baptists?"

Amanda apparently knew what this meant. She slid the mask back onto Colin's face and answered, "The Southern Baptist Convention just came out with an affirmation of the spiritual integrity of the BrainTrust, though they deplore some of the activities that take place here. They also denounced, let me see if I can quote this exactly, 'those who mistake personal belief for God's ultimate will, and apostatize true doctrine which is founded in tolerance for all beliefs.'"

Colin gurgled.

"So, pretty much as you had hoped."

Colin tilted his head and saw Dash. He pulled the mask down again. "Hey."

Amanda growled. "Shush. You're in no condition to be talking. You're gonna be here for a while." After pushing his mask back up, she turned to Dash. "You, on the other hand, will be leaving in a couple of days."

Dash rolled her eyes to look at her. "So quickly?"

"We'll give you a diagnostic bot to go home with you. It'll keep stats on you so detailed that I'll know as much about your condition by looking at my cell phone app as I could tell by looking at the monitors in this room. And I'll be able to administer drugs and give you orders just as easily. If you're at home, you'll be more likely to follow orders," she glared at Jam and Ping, "since you'll have people looking in on you."

Jam nodded. "That will work."

Ping concurred. "Oh goodie, I get to stick needles in you." She had a thought. "Is Dash still in danger? Should I get my Big Gun from the armory?"

Colin pulled his mask down, asked "Moving?" and put the mask back on before Amanda could complain.

Amanda nodded. "Yes. We're going out past the two-hundred-mile coastal limit of the Exclusive Economic Zone to international waters. We'll have more warning if someone tries to attack us again."

Colin shook his head and popped his mask long enough to say, "So Ping can shoot back."

Ping jumped on it. "I really need my Big Gun."

Amanda chose to not to hear them. Speaking to Dash, she continued, "You'll recover faster at home, even with these two as lookouts." She looked at Ping and pursed her lips. "Until Dash goes home, she needs guards. Jam, Ping, your duty station is here. Watch over her."

She looked back at Dash. "On a more pleasant topic, I saw in your medical history that you have a problem with the cartilage in your left knee. As it happens, we have another researcher whose experimental procedure might be able to fix you." She pulled a screen attached to an arm from the ceiling and configured it to show a video of a procedure on a knee.

Dash studied it silently as it ran, and as it concluded, looked at Amanda. "I believe this can be improved upon."

Colin once again chortled and pulled off his oxygen mask. "And that is why—"

Amanda shoved the mask back over his face with possibly excessive force. "No. You will not say it. Silence."

Dash opened her mouth to speak.

Amanda's finger swung to Dash. "You shouldn't be talking either. Silence." Dash closed her mouth.

Amanda arched an eyebrow at Ping. "No Big Gun without further authorization." Her eyes softened slightly as they looked at Jam, as if Amanda thought that Jam might, unlike the others, have some of the maturity of an adult. "Keep them under control." Her voice sounded so much like a sergeant's command that Jam instinctively straightened and snapped off a sharp salute, jerking in pain as she completed the maneuver. Amanda put her hands on her hips as she surveyed the scene one more time. "Well. I seem to have gotten the last word. Finally!"

And with that she strutted from the room.

The End

AUTHOR NOTES

It's been eighteen years since I last published a novel. Much has changed. But honestly, much of the change was easy enough to anticipate. The Skyhunter drone described in David's Sling in 1989 is now called a Predator. The online economy in that book is now called Amazon and eBay. The palmtop described in EarthWeb in 1999, used in the transformational event referred to in the story as the TopDrop, is now called a Samsung Galaxy. People still email to accuse me of having invented FaceBook. They also email to ask for guidance on how to create a Decision Duel, perhaps the most important tech I ever described that was never built.

Sometimes change is sudden—starkly nonlinear, like falling off a cliff. We all fell off such a cliff on November 8, 2016.

Much of my work is near-term extrapolation: given what we have, casting aside the fact that tech change is exponential, what might things look like in twenty years?

In January of 2016, the BrainTrust would not have been credible as a work of extrapolative sf. It would have been viewed as stupidly unrealistic. On November 9, after the election of Donald Trump, the BrainTrust future looked not only possible but almost mundanely mainstream.

I still don't expect the 101st Airborne to drop into Silicon Valley. But the possibility that the engineering teams that create the industries and jobs of the future will be destroyed by government meddling is no longer even a full standard deviation away from straightforward expectations. Similarly the ban on robots, which may seem ridiculous to a mainstream American, is already a matter of serious discussion in France. When the populists of both the Red and Blue parties realize that automation is the force of creative destruction behind the elimination of eighty percent of manufacturing jobs, will they make common cause to follow in France's footsteps? Why not?

The rest of Harmony of Enemies is also well within a standard deviation of what one might expect in the near future. People think that cruise liners are extraordinarily expensive, and a fleet of fourteen big ones would be just too crazily costly to be built for the sake of autonomy. Such ships are in fact quite expensive, but compared to rental apartments in Tokyo they look like bargains. Similarly medical tourism to evade the long lines and high costs of Western civilization is already a burgeoning industry today. Its marriage to the cruise liner industry is at this point almost inevitable.

An astonishing amount of work has been done on systems that look a lot like the BrainTrust archipelago. For an upbeat factual read about that part of our future, I recommend the book SeaSteading by Joe Quirk and Patri Friedman. It provided most of the background tech for the BrainTrust.

The only thing preventing us from building a Brain-Trust right now is the lack of a satisfactory power plant. I have brazenly stolen the design for the BrainTrust's nukes from TransAtomic, a startup company founded by MIT students and led by Dr. Leslie Dewan, who inadvertently helped me write the passages about the reactor in a brief email exchange we shared.

The TransAtomic reactor is a highly evolved derivative of the first molten salt nuclear reactor build by Oak Ridge National Laboratory back in the 60s. That's right, forty years ago we knew how to build small cheap inherently safe nuclear reactors. All we ever really had to do to solve global warming was use the tech we already had, before we forgot it all.

But that is another story.

Marc Stiegler

September 13, 2017

BOOKS BY MARC STIEGLER

The Braintrust - A Harmony of Enemies (1)
  (Prometheus Award Nominee)

The Braintrust: A Crescendo Of Fire (2)

Valentina
  (Hugo Award Finalist)

David's Sling
  (Prometheus Award Finalist)

EarthWeb

The Gentle Seduction (anthology)

CONNECT

Join the BrainTrust discussion group on Facebook at

https://www.facebook.com/groups/326423271191445/

Made in the USA
San Bernardino, CA
10 August 2018